The Sign in the Smoke

Read all the mysteries in the
NANCY DREW DIARIES

Nancy Drew

DIARIES™

The Sign in the Smoke

#12

CAROLYN KEENE

Aladdin
NEW YORK   LONDON   TORONTO   SYDNEY   NEW DELHI

This book is a work of fiction. Any references to historical events, real people, or real places are used fictitiously. Other names, characters, places, and events are products of the author's imagination, and any resemblance to actual events or places or persons, living or dead, is entirely coincidental.

ALADDIN

An imprint of Simon & Schuster Children's Publishing Division

1230 Avenue of the Americas, New York, NY 10020

This Aladdin paperback edition May 2016

Text copyright © 2016 by Simon & Schuster, Inc.

Cover illustration copyright © 2016 by Erin McGuire

Also available in an Aladdin hardcover edition.

All rights reserved, including the right of reproduction in whole or in part in any form.

ALADDIN is a trademark of Simon & Schuster, Inc., and related logo is a registered trademark of Simon & Schuster, Inc.

NANCY DREW, NANCY DREW DIARIES, and related logo are trademarks of Simon & Schuster, Inc.

For information about special discounts for bulk purchases, please contact Simon & Schuster Special Sales at 1-866-506-1949 or business@simonandschuster.com.

The Simon & Schuster Speakers Bureau can bring authors to your live event. For more information or to book an event contact the Simon & Schuster Speakers Bureau at 1-866-248-3049 or visit our website at www.simonspeakers.com.

Cover designed by Karin Paprocki

Interior designed by Mike Rosamilia

The text of this book was set in Adobe Caslon Pro.

Manufactured in the United States of America 0817 OFF

4 6 8 10 9 7 5

Library of Congress Control Number 2015948005

ISBN 978-1-4814-3817-9 (hc)

ISBN 978-1-4814-3816-2 (pbk)

ISBN 978-1-4814-3818-6 (eBook)

Contents

Dear Diary,

NO ONE LOVES WARM WEATHER MORE than me! But since trouble seems to find me even when the sun's glaring down, my summers usually aren't so relaxing. I decided that this year, however, all that would change. I was going to take a much-needed *self-imposed* summer break from sleuthing!

So when Bess suggested that she, George, and I sign up as counselors at Camp Cedarbark, I thought it was a great idea. I figured I'd spend time with the kids, make a few new friends, maybe even pick up a hobby. Of course, I should have known that escaping mystery-fueled drama is never as easy as it seems. . . .

CHAPTER ONE

A Summer Retirement

BESS PEERED DOWN INTO HER CUP AND THEN thrust it back at the girl who'd handed it to her. "Could I get just a *smidge* more marshmallow?"

"*More* marshmallow?" her cousin George asked, swirling her plastic spoon through her own pile of Strawberry Cheesecake Explosion. "If you get any more marshmallow, Bess, all of your organs are going to stick together."

My boyfriend, Ned, cleared his throat. "I'm pretty sure that's not how the human digestive system works," he said, watching as the ice cream scooper handed the cup back to Bess, "but you *are* going to have the mother of sugar highs."

Bess tilted her head at him. "After eating an ice cream sundae? You don't say." She smiled at the ice cream scooper, plunged her spoon into a fluffy cloud of marshmallow, and shoveled it into her mouth, closing her eyes in pleasure. "Ohhhh, yeah. That's the stuff. Besides"—she opened her eyes—"we're celebrating here. At least, Nancy, George, and I are. Aren't we?"

"We sure are," I agreed, stepping up to the counter. "Can I get a strawberry sundae with Oreo chip and whipped cream?"

Ned smiled at me. "Good combination."

"Thanks," I said. "I spent all winter planning the ultimate sundae combo."

Bess took another bite of her sundae and moaned. "And we can spend *all day* eating ice cream now, guys," she said happily. "Because as of midnight last night, it's officially *summer*!"

"For twelve beautiful, short weeks," Ned put in.

Bess glared at him. "Buzzkill."

"And then comes fall," Ned said, taking a lick of his own rocky-road-with-sprinkles cone. "Then winter. It'll be snowing before we know it!"

"My *point* is," Bess said, raising her spoon in the air, "that we girls have three months of gorgeous weather stretching ahead of us. *Three months.* What are we going to do with it all?"

I took my sundae from the ice cream scooper and handed over my money. "Um, if I were to guess? I'll probably end up solving a mystery or something."

"You're so predictable, Nance," George scoffed, rolling her eyes.

I took a bite of my sundae. *Ooh*, it was perfect. I'd done it. I'd created the ultimate sundae. "I dunno," I said, shrugging at George. "Maybe I'll take the summer off from solving mysteries. Take up knitting or something."

Now it was Bess's turn to roll her eyes.

"What?" I asked.

"I'll believe that when I see it, is all," she explained. "How are you going to manage it? Mysteries tend to find you, you know. I think the only way you could pull that off is to stop talking to people at all."

George nodded, chewing on a nugget of cheesecake. "Or go on a really long trip," she added.

"Where you don't speak the language," Ned put in, pausing from licking his cone.

"You *guys*!" I said, getting frustrated. "I'm serious. I mean, kind of."

"You want to stop solving mysteries?" Bess asked, looking incredulous. She slapped a hand over my forehead. "Are you feeling okay?"

I dodged out from under her. "Not *permanently*," I said. "But it might be nice to just relax this summer. Enjoy nature. Maybe play some sports."

I expected Bess to laugh again, but instead she looked thoughtful. "I think George might be right," she said slowly. "I think to do that, you might have to leave town. And I have an idea!" She put her sundae down on a nearby table and then swung her purse off her shoulder so she could start digging in it. Normally this was a twenty-minute process, minimum, so George and I looked at each other and sat down to continue eating our ice cream. But just as I had the perfect mouthful of strawberries, ice cream, and whipped cream, Bess pulled out a glossy brochure and waved it at me.

"Um," I said, struggling to swallow what I had in my mouth, "okay."

I took the brochure. The cover showed a beautiful lake surrounded by woods and cabins, and blocky text spelled out CAMP CEDARBARK.

I raised an eyebrow at Bess. "I think we're a little old for summer camp, don't you think?"

Bess, who'd sat down with us and was inhaling her sundae, sighed. "Not as *campers*," she said. "As *counselors*. Think about it, Nance. You want to relax, enjoy nature, maybe play some sports?"

"Yeah." George snorted. "There's nothing more relaxing than looking after six children who belong to someone else all summer long!"

Bess frowned at her. "Shush. You like kids." She turned back to me. "And it wouldn't be for the whole summer. Camp Cedarbark does little mini-sessions, each one week long! Besides, it's not just any camp, Nancy. I used to go there when I was a kid!"

I squinted at the brochure. "I thought you went to Camp Lark-something?"

"Camp Larksong," Bess confirmed. "But they closed five years ago, two years after my last visit! Now a Camp Larksong alum has finally bought the place and restored it. They sent this brochure to all the former Camp Larksong campers, encouraging us to get involved or send our kids."

"Kids?" asked Ned.

Bess shrugged. "Well, Camp Larksong was in business for twenty-three years, so . . ." She turned to me, her face as eager as a puppy's. "What do you think?"

I raised my eyebrows. "You're serious?"

"Why wouldn't I be?" Bess stuck out her lower lip in a pout. "I have so many happy memories of this place! I was sort of thinking of applying to be a counselor on my own, but it would be so much more fun with you guys!"

George looked at her cousin. "You really think I

could take care of a bunkful of children and not lose my mind?"

"You'd have *help*," Bess admonished her. "We'd each be assigned a CIT, counselor-in-training, who's a few years younger. And of course, we'd all be there to help each other. Besides"—she pointed an accusing finger at George—"you *like* children. You're a great babysitter! Remember when you watched cousin Gemma for the day and taught her how to code?"

George's lips turned up. "Well, *she* was an exceptional kid. She had a natural talent!"

"I guess we'd have activities to keep them busy, George," I said, trying to imagine the three of us relaxing by the lake in the photo. "It's not like we'd be starting from scratch."

"And the activities are *really fun*," Bess went on. "I know neither of you went to summer camp, but it's the greatest! Swimming and hiking and playing capture the flag and . . ."

I looked at George. Bess was right, I'd never been to summer camp . . . but it *did* sound really fun. And definitely more exciting than sitting in our backyard rereading Harry Potter with my feet in a kiddie pool, which was basically last summer. (When I wasn't sleuthing, that is.) "It would only be a week or two," I said quietly.

Bess looked at me, her eyes bulging in excitement as she realized she'd gained an ally. "Ten days," she squealed. "The mini-sessions are just one week of camp, and three days' training. That's not so bad, right? Even if you hated it, it's *only* ten days."

The silence that followed was broken by a *crunch!* We all turned to see Ned finishing up his waffle cone. "I'm sold," he said after he swallowed. "But unfortunately, I'm using the summer to bang out my science requirements. You're on your own, Nance."

Bess smiled at him. "You weren't invited anyway," she said. "It's a girls' camp. What do you say?" she asked, looking eagerly from me to George.

"I'm . . . *in*," I said, smiling in spite of myself. A week at camp! It was the last way I thought I'd spend my summer, and yet it was somehow perfect.

I looked back down at the photo on the brochure. It looked . . . *peaceful*.

Bess squealed and turned to George, squeezing her arm. "It's on you, cuz," she said, looking George in the eye. "You *know* this would be fun. Come on. Everything I suggest for us turns out to be fun!"

I held up my hand. *"Actually . . ."*

Ned raised a finger in the air. "Yeah, I'm gonna have to object to that one too."

George laughed.

Bess pretended to glare at me. "We're still all *alive*, anyway," she pointed out. Then she turned back to George. "Cuz, will you make my summer? Come on, say you're in."

George took the brochure from me and looked down at the photo. A slow smile crept across her face. "Okay," she said. "But if I get a bunkful of princessy mean girls, I am *coming for you in the night*, Bess."

"I can live with that," she said quickly. "I'm fast. I know how to hide. Anyway, *yay!*" She grabbed me suddenly around the waist with one hand, pulling in

George with the other. "Group hug! We're headed back to Camp Larksong!"

Six weeks and endless application forms later, I sat on my bed, cramming in my last two T-shirts into my camp duffel bag. Our housekeeper, Hannah, had helped me sew labels bearing my name onto all my clothes. Eight shirts, six pairs of shorts, two pairs of jeans, pj's, one casual dress—I was officially ready to go!

And not a minute too soon, because as soon as I zipped up my bag, I heard the toot of Bess's horn in the driveway. I hefted my bag onto my shoulder—*whoa, I hope I don't have to carry this far*—and maneuvered it down the stairs and into the front hall. Dad and Hannah, having heard the horn too, were standing there waiting to say good-bye.

Dad grinned at me. "I can't believe you're going to *camp*," he said, shaking his head. "You were never a *camp* type. You were a stick-your-nose-in-a-book type."

"It looks really fun, Dad," I said. "Besides, it's a

great excuse to spend some time outside and get to know some new people."

He nodded. "I know you'll have fun," he said, and leaned in for a hug.

"Don't forget to eat," Hannah advised as I finished up Dad's hug and went to hug her. "You'll be running around a lot!"

I chuckled. "Well, I can guarantee the food won't be as good as yours," I promised. "I'll miss you both. Write to me?"

Dad pulled out some folded paper and a preaddressed envelope from his shirt pocket. "Ready to go," he promised. "Don't worry, you won't miss any of the big news from River Heights."

"I love you both," I said, opening the door and squeezing through with my bag.

"Love you, too. Have fun," Dad said, leaning out to take the door from me and waving in Bess's direction. "Don't get in too much trouble."

I grinned back at him. "When have *I* ever gotten in trouble?"

I hauled my bag out to Bess's coupe and loaded it into the trunk, then climbed into the passenger seat. Bess was all smiley and pumped up, and couldn't stop talking about all the fun we were going to have at Camp Cedarbark. She explained that at Camp Larksong, each week ended with a special campout on a hill by the lake, with a sunset sing-along and ghost stories around the campfire. She'd read on Camp Cedarbark's website that they were planning to continue the tradition.

We swung by George's house, where she was waiting in the driveway with her parents. After lots of hugs and kisses (George is an only child, and her parents *love* her), George climbed into the backseat and we were off.

"Aren't you *excited*?" Bess asked, peering at her cousin in the rearview mirror when we were stopped at a traffic light. "Aren't we going to have the *best time ever*?"

"Yeeeeeeah," said George slowly. But she didn't look like she thought we were going to have the *best time ever*. She looked a little . . . concerned.

"Is something up?" I asked.

"Not exactly," she said. But she still wore a confused expression. "It's just . . . I Googled 'Camp Larksong' and 'Camp Cedarbark' last night."

The light changed, and Bess punched the gas with a little too much force. We lurched forward. "Don't tell me you found some nasty review," she said. "I've been looking at them every few weeks myself. Everyone says they've had an amazing time there."

"It wasn't a nasty review," George said, shaking her head. "It was a newspaper article. The headline was 'Tragedy Closes Camp Larksong.' It was dated five years ago—the year you said the camp closed."

Bess frowned. "That's strange. I never heard about any tragedy. What did the article say?"

George hesitated. "That's just the thing—I couldn't access the article. It was taken down a year ago. I just found a link to the cached page."

Bess looked thoughtful as she pulled onto the highway. Camp Cedarbark was about two hours away from River Heights. For a moment, we were all silent as she merged into traffic and we all thought our separate thoughts.

"I'm sure it's nothing," Bess said after a minute or two, startling me. "If there were really some big tragedy, I would have heard about it, right? I kept in touch with some of my fellow campers for years. Nobody mentioned anything."

"I guess," George said, but she was staring out the window with a pensive expression.

Things got quiet again for a while, and I tried to lose myself in the landscape whooshing by and ignore the little worried voice inside my head.

The voice that said, *Please don't let there be a mystery to solve at Camp Cedarbark!*

CHAPTER TWO

~❧~

Welcome to Camp

"WELCOME, COUNSELORS!"

A woman in her early twenties with long, frizzy blond hair and green eyes stepped up to the stage and grabbed the microphone. I dropped my fork back into my spaghetti, startled, and looked around at the other counselors.

"That's Deborah Jackson, the camp director," the person across from me, a dark-haired petite girl whose name I hadn't gotten, whispered to the table.

I nodded slowly. I was feeling overwhelmed. We'd just pulled up the driveway of Camp Cedarbark—which, so far, looked as beautiful as it had in the photos—when a girl wearing a baseball cap had run up to the car, told Bess to park it in the "employee parking lot," and instructed us to come into the mess hall immediately after—while we'd been stuck in traffic, dinner had already started.

We'd barely had time to grab our bags and pile them in the mess hall foyer for now. Dinner was spaghetti with meatballs and salad—Bess told us that about 70 percent of a camper's diet is made up of spaghetti—served with "bug juice," or some kind of red fruit punch. The food wasn't exactly gourmet, but I was starving, so it tasted great.

Now the counselors around us all started applauding, so I looked around at my friends and then joined in.

"Welcome to Camp Cedarbark," the woman—Deborah—went on. "We've been having a fantastic summer so far, and this week promises to be no exception! Thank you all so much for applying to be counselors for our Best of All Worlds camp—this week, instead of focusing on one activity, like arts and crafts or sports, our campers will get to try it all! And so will you." She paused. "But of course, you won't have to do it alone. You'll all be leading a bunk of six campers, but you'll each be assigned a CIT, a counselor-in-training, to help you. The CITs will arrive in two days and will have one day of training with you before the campers arrive. Make no mistake, though, *you* ladies are in charge. I expect you to all be responsible, and to remember that these girls' parents have entrusted their precious children to you. Let's make sure everybody is safe and happy—and if you have any concerns, you can always speak to me or my husband, Miles. Miles, wave at everyone!"

A stout, bearded man wearing an orange Camp Cedarbark shirt walked out from the corner and waved. We all clapped politely.

Deborah went on, "After dinner, we're going to spend a couple of hours learning child CPR with our resident nurse, Cathy. Then you'll get a chance to relax and unwind at the campfire. But don't stay up too late—breakfast is *promptly* at seven thirty every morning."

Next to me, George groaned.

Deborah waved. "All right, enjoy your dinner!"

The next two hours went by in a blur. We finished our spaghetti and bused our tables, then helped fold up the tables and roll them to the side of the room. Then we sat down with Cathy, a kind-eyed lady with short, curly gray hair, who brought out two child-size dummies and taught us the basics of child CPR. We practiced with partners—mine was Sam, the baseball-cap-wearing girl who'd greeted us in the driveway, who seemed super nice. Then, as we were all getting worn out, Cathy finally collected the dummies and said that was enough for now—we'd practice again tomorrow. She told us to leave the mess hall and walk toward the lake, where Deborah and Miles would have started the campfire.

We stumbled out of the mess hall and, in the moonlight, found our way past a row of cabins, down a small, steep path, and to a big campfire area that was right on the bank of the lake. Eight big logs surrounded a fire that was ringed by rocks. It was huge and crackly, and behind it, Deborah and Miles sat on one of the logs, smiling.

"We're so happy you're all here," Miles said. "Make yourselves comfortable, please. Your work is done for tonight."

Once we were all settled around the campfire, Miles pulled out an acoustic guitar and began playing. He asked whether there were any Camp Larksong alums there, and Bess eagerly raised her hand. Looking around the campfire, I counted two others.

"That's great," said Miles. "Deborah is an alum too."

"Five years in a row," Deborah confirmed. "First as a camper, then a CIT, then a counselor. That's why we bought and restored this place. I just love it so much."

Miles fingered a few notes on the guitar, and the alums all made little noises of recognition.

"Who remembers the camp song?" Deborah asked. She began singing in a clear voice:

Friends and nature, sports and fun,
Camp Larksong glitters in the sun,

We come together every year,

Some come from far, some come from near. . . .

Bess began singing along beside me, and soon the others who'd raised their hands to say they were alums joined in. The song was folksy and pretty, and it made me a little sleepy, but I could also see how happy the alums were to sing it.

From the Camp Larksong song, Miles moved on to "Kumbaya," and then "On Top of Spaghetti," and then I lost track. We all chimed in singing song after song, as the moon rose high over the lake and the sky got darker and darker.

After the seventh or eighth song, Miles lifted his guitar and stood. "I think that'll do it for Deborah and me!" he said.

Deborah smiled and stood up too. "We were up at five today getting the camp all ready for you," she said, a little apologetically. "As long as you keep the noise down, feel free to stay out here for a while and get to know one another. Until the CITs arrive, you'll all be sleeping in Pine Cabin, which is the long, low one over by the mess hall. You passed it on your way here."

Everyone said good night, and Deborah and Miles disappeared into the woods.

"So who is everybody again?" asked the dark-haired girl who'd spoken up at dinner. "The last few hours have been such a blur."

We all reintroduced ourselves. There were eight of us: me; George; Bess; Sam, who was going to be the sports counselor; Bella, the dark-haired girl; Maddie, a willowy redhead; Taylor, a soft-spoken, round girl who said she was the arts and crafts counselor; and Charla, a cheery dark-eyed girl with tiny braids.

We all talked about where we were from, and what had inspired us to come here. Most of the other girls were from closer to the camp. Bella even lived in the same town. "I get to go really far away for my summer vacation," she said, rolling her eyes. But she explained that she was a Camp Larksong alum (she'd started coming after Bess stopped), and she'd always wanted to come back.

When all the introductions were over, Bella made a big show of checking to make sure she couldn't see Deborah and Miles, and then turned back to us. "So," she said in a mischievous voice, "is anyone scared to be here?"

"Why would we be?" I blurted.

Charla looked confused too. "Away from home, you mean?" she asked. "Or out in the woods? I *am* kind of scared of bears."

"*No*," Bella said, sounding a little impatient, "I mean *here*. On this site. You know, the old Camp Larksong."

There was silence for a minute, and then George looked at her skeptically. "Is this about the 'tragedy'?" she asked. "I heard something happened here, but I couldn't find out much more than that."

"Yeah, 'tragedy,' that's one way to put it," Bella said.

I felt a shiver run up my spine. "What's another way?" I asked, wishing she'd get to the point.

"Well." Bella's eyes widened and her face seemed to come alive. "Five years ago, the last year Camp Larksong was open, they had the Best of All Worlds camp—just like the one we're here for."

"Okay," said Taylor. "So?"

"On the last night," Bella went on, "they took their tents and sleeping bags and headed out to Hemlock Hill for the campout by the lake—a Camp Larksong tradition."

"I remember," said Maddie, who was the third alum. "It was always the most fun night of camp . . . though I barely got any sleep!"

Bella widened her eyes even farther. "Well, *this* night, something really crazy happened! The rumor is one of the counselors went nuts. . . ." She paused for dramatic effect.

"And did *what?*" George demanded finally. I could tell Bella's milking of the story was driving *her* nuts.

"And she *drowned* one of her *own* campers in the lake!" Bella finished. "You guys, this place is legit haunted. Everyone in Potterville knows that. We're always seeing weird lights in the woods, a wailing sound coming from the lake. . . ."

Taylor looked horrified. "She *drowned* one of her campers?" she asked. "Yeah, that would make me pretty mad! I would totally haunt this place if someone *drowned* me."

Maddie nodded slowly, looking down into her lap. "I heard about this too, from a friend from camp I used to write to," she said. "I didn't want to believe it was true. But—"

"We don't know it's true," George cut in. Her voice was as sharp and no-nonsense as ever. I found it kind of comforting. "And to be honest, I kind of doubt it."

Bella glared at her. "Why do you doubt it?" she asked. "Are you calling me a liar?"

George shook her head. "No, no. I believe *you* believe it. But . . . guys, drowning someone is murder. I've Googled this place a few times. I'm sure some of you have too. Don't you think, if a murder actually happened here, it would have ended up in the news somewhere?"

"Maybe the camp covered it up," said Bella.

"Yeah," Maddie whispered. "I'm sure they wouldn't have wanted anyone to know."

Whoooooooooooooo! We all jumped as a sudden wailing

traveled over the water from the other side of the lake.

"That was an owl," George said.

But Bess looked unconvinced. She bit her lip. "The camp *did* close down kind of suddenly," she said. "I always wondered why. If something like this happened . . ."

George gave her a doubtful look. "Bess, come on."

"Come on *what?*" Bella said. "She's not allowed to believe me either? What is she, your dog?"

Bess scowled at Bella, clearly annoyed. "She's my *cousin,*" she said. "She doesn't tell me what to do. But I am interested in her opinion." Bess got to her feet. "Look, nobody can prove anything tonight. So that was an interesting story, Bella, but that's all it is right now—a story." She yawned and covered her mouth. "I'm really tired, and I think we have to get up at some ungodly hour to make breakfast tomorrow. Anyone else ready to turn in?"

"Me," George said without hesitation, getting up.

"Me too," said Sam, slowly getting to her feet.

Soon most of the others followed. Bella was the last to stand, and did so reluctantly. I could tell by the look in her eye that she wasn't pleased by how this conversation had turned out. But why? I wondered. Was she hoping to bond with the others over this ghost tale? I was with George on this one—it was super creepy to think about the camp closing because someone had died here, but Bella's story sounded far-fetched.

"Let's go to bed," I agreed. "I'm sure we have a busy day ahead of us."

Pine Cabin was basically a rustic pine box. Six metal bunk beds lined the walls, and there was a separate bathroom with a few stall showers and toilets. We laid our sleeping bags out. George and Bess shared one bunk, so I asked Taylor if she wanted to share, and she said yes. We were all sleepy, so we didn't take long to change into our pj's, use the bathroom, brush our teeth, and climb into bed.

I had the top bunk. "Good night, guys," I called as I sleepily burrowed into the pillow I'd brought from home. It smelled of Hannah's favorite lavender-scented detergent.

"Good night, Nancy," came seven voices back to me.

I dreamed I had to go to the bathroom, but I was up in a tree, and the bathroom was down on the ground. I had to climb down the thick pine branches to get back to earth, but they were too tangled, and it was too confusing. Meanwhile the pressure was building, and I was getting really worried I wasn't going to make it! The dream seemed to go on forever until suddenly my eyes popped open and there I was, staring at the ceiling of Pine Cabin, desperately having to pee.

I scrambled down as quickly as I could without stepping on Taylor and ran to use the bathroom.

Hugely relieved, I finished up and was walking back to my bed when I heard it.

WHOOOOOOOO-WOOOOO-HOOOOOOO!

I felt like ice water had been poured into my veins. It was coming from just outside the cabin. It was kind of like the sound that had come across the lake—the "owl" sound, according to George. But this was much louder, and closer.

WOOOOOO-HOOOO-WOOOOOOOO!

"What the heck?" Sam's confused voice came from one of the bunks to my right, and I turned toward it.

"You hear it too?"

She sat up. "Yeah, I can hear that. I'm pretty sure the whole camp can hear it."

"It's loud, right?"

"It sounds like it's coming from right outside."

There was a creak from the bunks across the room.

"What *is* that?" Bess asked.

"I'm not sure," I said honestly.

Wooooooooooohh . . .

This time the sound was softer, almost pretty. More of a whisper than a wail.

"Should we go outside and check it out?" Sam asked. Now that I could see her face, she looked terribly annoyed.

I glanced out the small window. It was dark outside,

but cool blue moonlight shone down on the clearing that surrounded the mess hall. I didn't see anything unusual. But the thought of going out there was not appealing.

More creaking. Bess got up from her bed and walked over to us. She grabbed a flashlight from her duffel bag. "I think we have to go," she said.

"Where are you going?" a sleepy voice asked from behind her. George.

"Outside," Bess said. "To check out—"

Wooooooooo–wooooooooo!

There was an abrupt *thunk* as George jumped down from her bed. "What on earth . . . ," she muttered.

I got my flashlight too, and so did Sam. As we approached the door, I couldn't help asking, "Do you think it could be the ghost?"

I was normally much more logical than this. But it was the middle of the night, in a cabin, in the woods.

I was surprised when no one said *no* right away.

"I don't want to think about it," Bess murmured.

"We're going to be here for nine more days." She was the only one to respond.

We pushed open the heavy wooden door and walked outside.

Wooooooooooooooooo!

It was coming from the woods . . . from the path toward the lake.

We crept toward the woods. Closer . . . and closer. My skin felt too tight and my heart beat a jumpy rhythm in my chest.

"How far do we go?" Bess whispered.

"Far enough to figure out what this is," Sam replied.

It was cooler outside than it had been during the campfire, and an even cooler breeze seemed to come down the path from the lake. I knew it was probably just air cooled from skimming over the lake's surface, but it felt . . . *ghostly.*

I couldn't help wondering what it would feel like to drown. Feeling the air leave your body and knowing you would never take another breath. What if someone was holding you down when you were trying to break free of the surface . . . if someone went crazy and drowned you, like Bella had said? What would it feel like to be held underwater and know you were dying?

"*Wooooooooo* . . . BOO!"

"*AAAAAUUUUUUUUGH!*"

I let out an ear-piercing scream as a pale figure jumped out from behind a tree. Bess, George, and Sam were screaming too. But instead of wailing at us some more, or grabbing us with its ghostly hands, the figure abruptly stopped wailing and started cracking up. When I was over my shock, I turned to look at her.

Bella!

"Were you *scared*?" she asked, a smug look on her face. "Bet you believe my story now, huh?"

"What the heck, Bella!" Sam cried, putting her hands on her hips. "This was all a joke? Do you think this is funny? We have to get up in, like, three hours!"

Bella's lip twisted. "Chill, guys," she said, folding her arms and glancing toward the clearing. "It was just a prank! I thought you'd been to camp before." She looked at Bess.

Bess frowned. "I've been to camp before," she said, "but pranks are usually funny."

George, who wore a deep frown and had seemed to be thinking something over this whole time, suddenly spoke. "Did you make up that whole dumb story?" she asked. "About the counselor drowning the girl? Was it just the setup to your prank to scare us?"

Bella turned to George, surprised. Then her expression hardened into a cold, steely glare. "I'm not telling," she said. "I guess you'll just have to wait and see, hmmm?"

"Well, I'm going to 'wait and see' back in bed," Sam said, turning her flashlight toward the cabin. "This was stupid, and I'm exhausted."

Sam led the way back to the cabin, and Bess fell into step behind her, then George. After a moment, Bella scowled, shook her head, and followed behind George toward the cabin, folding her arms more tightly around her.

I couldn't help but glance one more time down the path that led to the lake. Another chilly breeze blew, sending a chill up my spine.

I wasn't totally sure Bella had made up the story. But I wasn't so sure I wanted to wait to find out, either.

CHAPTER THREE

~❧~

A Shadowy Surprise

I WASN'T SURE WHETHER IT WAS BECAUSE of Bella's prank, but the next morning I felt tired and out of sorts. It was still a little chilly outside, and the shorts and T-shirt I'd packed did little to keep me warm. Sam encouraged me to tough it out, because it would be warming up later. But I couldn't help wishing I was back in bed—at home.

Things only got worse when Deborah announced our morning activity. "Swimming tests!" she said enthusiastically at breakfast. "These are very important to judge your comfort level in the water, and how much supervision your campers will need while they're at the lake."

Normally I enjoyed swimming—but I was very much a "splash around in the shallow end" kind of girl, and nowhere near lifeguard level. I knew how to swim, but I wasn't great at it. I couldn't hold my breath very long. And I tired out easily.

After breakfast, we all went back to Pine Cabin and put on our bathing suits. Mine was a simple green one-piece I'd had for eons. I pulled on a hooded sweat-shirt as a cover-up, but I knew it was only a temporary comfort—I'd soon be plunged in the cool lake.

As we were about to leave the cabin, Taylor suddenly let out a moan. She clutched her stomach and went running for the bathroom, and after a few seconds we could hear retching.

"Uh-oh," said Sam, wide-eyed.

"I'll go check on her," said Bess, and she disappeared into the bathroom.

A few minutes later we heard the water running, and then Taylor stepped out of the bathroom, supported by Bess. "I'm really sorry, guys," she said, looking pale. "I think breakfast didn't agree with me."

"You'd better stay here," Maddie said, gesturing to Taylor's bunk. "Lie down. We'll explain to Deborah and Miles."

"Thanks," Taylor murmured, diving into her sleeping bag.

After saying our good-byes and get wells, the rest of us headed to the lake. I was still shivering.

"You know, it's okay if you're not a *great* swimmer," Bess said as we were walking down the same path where Bella had pranked us the night before. "The camp has lifeguards. So, you know, no pressure."

I knew that was meant to comfort me.

Bella had barely spoken that morning, saying the minimum she had to in order to seem polite—*pass the muffins, thank you, oh, I'm fine, thanks.* Whether she was still miffed by the way we'd reacted, or whether she just sensed she needed to tone it down and give us all a break from her, I couldn't quite tell.

When we got to the lake, it was the brilliant

robin's-egg blue of the morning sky. I poked my toe into the water and shivered—it was also a good ten degrees colder than the morning air.

"Don't worry," Sam whispered when she saw me cringe, "you'll get used to it."

I knew she was right, but I'd still have to get out of the lake at some point. And *then* I'd be freezing!

"All right, girls," Deborah said, stepping onto a short wooden pier that stretched into the lake. She was wearing a red, white, and blue striped one-piece. "For the basic swimming test, we'll have you jump off the edge of this pier, swim out to the float, move about three yards away and tread water for two minutes, then swim back. This all must be completed in five minutes. Any counselor who passes this test will get their blue swimming badge, which allows you to swim in the lake as long as there's a lifeguard present. If anyone would like to take the lifeguard test, that wins you a red swimming badge, and you'll be allowed to swim in the lake unsupervised. Is anyone interested?"

Sam raised her hand, and so did Bella, after some hesitation.

"Great," said Deborah. "We'll save you two for last, then, since it's a more complicated test."

"Can I run to the ladies' room then?" Sam asked. "Sorry—I should have gone back at the cabin."

"Sure, that's fine," Deborah said. "There's an outhouse down a little path that leads off to the right, on your way back to the mess hall."

Sam turned and disappeared into the woods. But before Deborah could continue, Bella raised her hand.

"Yes, Bella?" Deborah asked.

"Can I go get a hoodie?" Bella asked. "I'm cold, and if we're just going to be waiting for a while . . ."

"Sure." Deborah shrugged. "Run back to the cabin quickly and then come right back, okay?"

"Okay." Bella nodded and then scampered back up the path.

"Now, let me demonstrate the basic test for you." Deborah walked out to the end of the pier, pinched her nose, and jumped in with a huge *SPLASH!*

"Ooh!" she shrieked when she came up for air. "That's brisk! Anyway, I'm going to swim over to the float like so. . . ." She began paddling, kicking her legs out behind. The lake water splashed into crystals all around her. It was a couple of minutes before she reached the float. "Okay!" she yelled, struggling to make her voice carry over the yards that separated her from the pier. "Now I'm going to—*aaugh!*"

In the blink of an eye, it looked like Deborah was suddenly yanked *downward*—into the lake! Where she'd floated a few seconds earlier, holding on to the float, was a little whirlpool of churning water.

I looked uneasily at George. "What just happened?"

George shook her head. "Do you think she's okay? Should we—"

But then the surface of the lake was broken again, and an extremely wet, slick-haired Deborah came up sputtering.

"Are you okay?" Maddie yelled, cupping her hands over her mouth.

Deborah held up one finger to say *wait one minute.*

She pushed her hair back from her face, still blinking and gasping—clearly whatever had pulled her down had surprised her, too.

"I'm okay," she said after a few seconds. "That was the darnedest thing! It felt like someone . . ." She looked down into the water, biting her lip.

"Someone did *what?*" Charla called, looking openly worried now.

Deborah frowned, peering beneath the surface of the water. I turned to look at George again, and she returned my glance with a furrowed brow. Nobody was saying it—but I knew we were all thinking of the story Bella had told the night before. The camper who'd drowned in this very lake. The camper who supposedly haunted the camp.

All at once, Deborah shook her head and turned back to us, smiling. "Nothing," she said. "Just ignore me! I'm sorry, folks, there are some reeds and plants down there, and my foot must have gotten snagged on one of them. No big deal!"

"What about *us?*" Charla murmured, too quietly

for Deborah to hear. "I don't want to get caught by any weed."

I swallowed hard. I wasn't proud to admit it, but I was thinking the same thing. I wasn't a terribly strong swimmer to begin with. The last thing I needed was some angry "weed" pulling me down.

If it really is a weed.

Deborah demonstrated the rest of the test: treading water for two minutes, then swimming back. Nothing else happened that would be considered out of the ordinary. When Deborah crested the ladder that led back up to the pier, she held out her arms for applause, and we all clapped politely.

"*Thank* you," said Deborah with a smile. "I deserve that, for being the first one to brave that cold water! Who's next? Let's see. . . ." She walked to the edge of the pier and picked up a clipboard. "Sam and Bella were interested in the lifeguard test, right? So let's do the basic tests first. Alphabetical order?" Without waiting for us to answer, she squinted at the paper on her clipboard. "Benson, Charla?"

Charla cringed, but nodded and bravely moved forward. In what seemed like no time, she'd jumped into the water and headed to the float. She passed her test with flying colors, and then Maddie took and passed hers. I was beginning to feel calm again when Deborah called out, "Drew, Nancy? I think you're up!"

Great. I raised my hand, trying to muster up a not-miserable expression.

Deborah smiled encouragingly. "Okay. A little advice from someone who's been there: jump in from the end of the pier. Rip off the Band-Aid, you know? You get used to the water faster that way."

I took a breath and glanced at Bess. *You. This was your idea.* But she just smiled like we were all having a great time. I strolled to the edge of the pier and bent my toes over. The water looked deep green up close, and I couldn't see much beyond the surface.

A shrill whistle sounded behind me. I cringed and turned around.

Deborah was holding up a whistle she'd looped around her neck and grinning. "Sorry," she said. "It's just, we have a lot of swim tests to get through. Maybe we should hur—"

She was right, I realized before she even finished. So I jumped.

Splash!

The water wasn't *too* cold. It just felt like I was being pelted with ice cubes by a bunch of angry polar bears. It made every part of my body want to shrivel, and I gasped so hard I had to remind myself to paddle and stay afloat.

Immediately my teeth started chattering. *Br-r-r-r-r-r. Br-r-r-r-r.*

All right, I thought, *let's get this over with!*

Deborah looked down at me from the pier and raised a stopwatch from her pocket. "Okay, start swimming for the raft!" she called.

I turned around, located the raft, and made a beeline there. Moving was good. Moving was better than being still, because the tiny bit of exercise warmed me a little.

By the time I reached the raft, I was feeling a little more confident. I slapped the side and turned around.

"Almost done!" Deborah shouted. "Now push off just a little ways—there! Good! Okay, I'm starting the timer. You tread water there until I tell you to stop!"

I moved my arms and legs, trying to do the minimum I needed to keep myself afloat. This was the part of the test I'd been dreading. Treading water always made me nervous. I was so aware of how tired I was getting, how my breath was becoming more labored. *How long can I really keep this up?* I'd never timed myself. I just hoped I had two minutes in me.

"One minute down!" Deborah shouted after what felt like forever. "One to go!"

I kept moving. *Treading, treading, treading* . . . I glanced at the shore and, at that moment, remembered that neither Sam nor Bella had returned to the lake from the bathroom or the cabin. *Hasn't it been long enough?* How long had Deborah's test taken, anyway? Surely it didn't take that long to—

"AAAAUUGH!"

Suddenly my head plunged under the surface and my eyes, nostrils, mouth, and ears filled with lake water. My throat burned and, in my shock, I gasped, letting the air out of my lungs. Something had grabbed my foot and yanked it down! I began choking and gagging, reflexively trying to pull my foot away from whatever held it, but it was no use. I tried to shimmy around, working up enough force to pry my foot away from whatever—*whoever?*—held it. After a few seconds, my eyes adjusted and I could see a few inches in front of me in the green, murky water. Deborah had been right—the floor of the lake was covered with long green plants. But that didn't feel like what had my foot.

I looked down at my leg and pulled again. What I saw made me gasp, which only made me swallow more lake water, gagging more. . . .

It looks like a human figure.

The water was too murky to make out much more than a shadow. But I could clearly see arms, legs, a head. This was no reed!

Terrified, I yanked one more time on my foot.

This time, it came free.

I didn't hesitate. I paddled my arms toward the surface, kicking behind me as hard as I could.

It was probably only a second or two before my head broke the surface of the water, but it felt like days. I gasped in a huge mouthful of air, which just pushed more water down my throat, making me gag again. But the air felt heavenly. I pushed my hair back from my forehead and blinked rapidly, trying to see.

When my vision returned, I saw Deborah watching me curiously from the pier. "Nancy, are you all right? That's exactly where I went down. There must be a reed. . . ."

I shook my head. "It wasn't a reed!" I called.

Deborah looked surprised. "No?" she asked. "Well, you probably can't be sure. Did you see—"

"It was a person!" I yelled. "I saw a figure underwater! It looked like a person!"

Deborah looked at me for a moment, confused, and then her expression hardened to a frown. Meanwhile, the other counselors behind her tittered and began whispering to one another. Bess and George exchanged a concerned glance and then both looked back at me, as if to say, *Really?*

That's when I realized how insane it sounded.

How would a person be able to breathe underwater? Where had he or she come from? What possible motive could he or she have to attack me—or maybe Deborah *and* me—under the water?

But as I remembered those terrible few seconds underwater, I was sure of it. I could see the curve of the figure's shoulder, feel its fingers on my ankle. They were *fingers* on my ankle. Not leaves or reeds. I was positive.

Wasn't I?

"We're having someone come out to trim the reeds at the bottom of the lake," Deborah announced at dinner that night. "We think this should address any problems we had during swim tests today." She glanced at me, and I looked down at my chicken nuggets.

No one believes me. I'm not sure I believe myself.

Deborah cleared her throat. "This means we won't

be having any swimming tomorrow, when the CITs arrive, which means we'll have to conduct their swim tests at the same time as the campers'—but that's probably all right. Better safe than sorry, I always say."

She put down the microphone and went to sit down at her table to finish dinner.

George took a sip of bug juice and then put down her cup, studying me across the table. "Could it have been your shadow you saw?" she asked, not even bothering to introduce the subject. We'd been talking about it on and off all afternoon.

I shrugged, picking up a french fry. "I don't think so," I said. "It looked like another person."

"But just . . . *how?*" Bess asked, chewing thoughtfully on a french fry herself.

I couldn't answer her question. I hadn't been able to answer it all day. What *would* another person be doing underwater? How could they breathe? What about—

Bella cleared her throat. "I think we all know how," she said in a low voice.

All eyes turned to her.

"Oh, come on, Bella," Taylor chided. She'd started feeling better after lunch and had been in training with us since then. "Not that old story again. We know that's something you just made up to scare us."

Bella scowled. "No, that's not what you know. That's what you *decided* to make yourselves feel better."

George tilted her head. "So it's just a coincidence?" she asked. "You told us this scary legend about the camp and then planned this awesome prank to freak us all out on the first night? I doubt it."

Bella glared at George and then turned to look at Maddie. "Maddie's heard it too," she pointed out. "Didn't you, Mad? You said that last night. You heard the story about the drowning too."

Maddie brought a forkful of carrots to her mouth and chewed deliberately, looking down at her tray. "I heard *something* happened here," she corrected.

"Something involving a drowning," Bella prodded.

"Something involving a camper," Maddie said, nodding. "And . . . the lake."

Everyone was silent for a minute. I felt Bella's eyes on me and looked up.

"Maybe what you saw in the lake," Bella said, standing up, "wasn't alive at all."

With that, she picked up her tray and stalked off.

CHAPTER FOUR

~

Standoff at the Lake

THE NEXT MORNING THE CITS BEGAN arriving at nine a.m., just after breakfast. As soon as the first car pulled up and the first grinning face emerged into the sunlight, the mood at the camp changed. We'd all been tense the night before, arguing about what had happened at the lake, whether I could be believed in the first place, what the figure could have been. By the time we went to sleep, long after lights-out, Taylor and Maddie seemed close to siding with Bella and believing that something supernatural was going on at the camp. George, unsurprisingly, flat-out refused to believe this, and Bess, Charla, Sam, and I were skeptics too. Still, I couldn't deny a little flutter of fear that went through me every time I remembered that shadow in the water.

It looked human. But how *could* it be?

You would think after solving so many cases in which "ghosts" ended up being, well, "not ghosts," I wouldn't believe in them.

But sometimes it's hard not to.

We all settled on a bench in front of the camp office to wait for our CITs. The first to arrive was assigned to Bess, and her name was Janie. She had a small, heart-shaped face and dark hair cut close to her jawline. She was smiley and enthusiastic about being at camp, but when it came time for her mom to leave, she was super reluctant to give up her smartphone.

"Oh man," she murmured. "I knew this was coming. . . . It's just . . . I've never been away from technology for a whole week!"

George smiled. "I know how you feel."

"I have a blog," Janie went on, "where I talk about new technological innovations and review some games and programs. I put up a post saying there'd be no updates for a week . . . but it's going to feel really weird!"

George poked Bess and whispered, "I like this girl. Want to trade?"

Bess shoved her away. "Mini-George is *mine*," she hissed. "You haven't even met yours yet."

Bess took Mini-George—*Janie*—over to the cabin Deborah assigned them to, Maple Shade Cabin, then moved her own things there from Pine Cabin. When the campers arrived tomorrow, they'd be presiding over a bunkful of eight-year-olds.

Next to arrive was Frankie, Maddie's curly-brown-haired CIT, and then Susie, who had silky dark hair and a serious expression. She was assigned to Bella.

"I hope I get someone good," George whispered to me as we continued to wait. "I liked that Janie."

"Remember what Mrs. Collins said in kindergarten,

George," I said. "You get what you get and you don't get upset. I'm sure we'll both get *great* CITs. And I'm personally going to need mine! I've never been alone in a room with six kids before."

"Hear, hear," George agreed, as a classic Mustang convertible pulled up.

The girl who climbed out of the passenger seat looked like she could have walked out of a movie from the 1960s. She wore a floral scarf knotted around her hair and big, round sunglasses. Once she'd taken out her duffel bag and placed it on the ground, she smiled and pulled off the scarf, revealing a cascade of wavy blond hair. "I'm Maya?" she asked. "Maya Beaumont? I'm going to be a CIT? I'm so excited! I came to this camp when I was teeny tiny!"

Deborah walked up and introduced herself, then looked at her clipboard. Just then a silver SUV pulled up, and out climbed a preppily dressed redhead with cool blue eyes. A single silver barrette held back her bangs, and she carried a Moleskine notebook, which looked well-loved.

"Excuse me," she said, as a middle-aged woman climbed out of the driver's side and popped the trunk. "I'm Marcie Polk? I'm supposed to be a CIT here."

George looked at me with raised eyebrows. But before I could respond, Maya the blonde came running over and threw her arms around me.

"I'm *so, so, so* excited!" she said. "Is your name Nancy? My name's Maya. I'm going to be your CIT and we're going to be in the Juniper Cabin with a bunkful of ten-year-olds! Isn't that *perfect*? Couldn't you just *die*? We're going to have so much fun! Have I mentioned I came to this camp when I was little?"

I smiled and introduced myself to Maya, saying that yes, that sounded pretty great, and that I was sure we were going to have a lot of fun. "I'm sure I'll need your help," I added. "I've never been a counselor before—I've never even been to camp! So you can show me the ropes."

Maya nodded eagerly. "Sure thing!"

As Maya grabbed her bag and explained which cabin was Juniper Cabin, at least as Deborah had explained it to her, George glanced at me and winked. "Have fun with Mini-Bess," she whispered.

At that moment Marcie walked up and opened her notebook. "Are you George?" she asked. "I'm Marcie. I'm going to be your CIT. Deborah says we'll be staying in Pine Cabin with the seven-year-olds?"

George looked a little panicked. "Hoo, boy," she said. "The youngest campers. That will be a challenge. I'm going to need your help, kid."

Marcie just nodded, seeming to take that in stride. She began flipping through her notebook. "I talked to my old Brownie troop leader to get some tips on dealing with kids of different ages," she said. "Do you want to go over what she said about seven-year-olds?"

As George raised her eyebrows, Maya turned around and whistled. "Wow, you're organized!" she said. When Marcie looked at her in surprise, Maya smiled and held out her hand. "I'm Maya. Sorry. I should introduce myself. I'm *so* excited to be here! I'm sure we're going to be great friends! Anyway, do you always carry that notebook?"

Marcie hesitated for just a moment before smiling. "Yeah, I do. I guess I'm really curious about people. I like to talk to them and then write down what they tell me. It's just this habit I have."

George bugged out her eyes and looked at me.

"Mini-Nancy," I whispered. "A complete set."

George shook her head as though she couldn't believe it. "All right, Min—I mean, Marcie." She smiled. "I'm sure we'll have more time to get to know one another at lunch. For now, though, we should probably get our stuff into Pine Cabin and start cleaning it up! Only"—she looked at her watch—"twenty-three hours until the campers arrive."

Marcie nodded. "That's plenty of time," she said. "I mean, if we're organized and stay focused."

Maya clapped her hands. "Only twenty-three hours, guys! I can't *wait*! This is going to be the best week ever!" She held up one hand, palm side out.

After a moment, Marcie slapped her five. "Best week ever," she agreed with a shy smile.

George and I followed suit. "Best week ever," I said,

feeling 100 percent better than I had before the CITs had arrived.

After we spent about an hour cleaning Juniper Cabin and getting it ready for the campers to arrive, the rest of the day was taken up by training, training, and more training, with breaks for lunch and dinner. We learned special Camp Cedarbark games like capture the flag and Shark Pit, we learned how to do trust falls, and we learned how to safely cook food over an open fire (useful for the end-of-camp campout!). We learned about fostering sportsmanship, stopping bullies, encouraging campers to resolve their own disagreements, and identifying problems a camper might have that would be too big for us to handle and should be referred to Deborah or Miles.

By the time we got back to Juniper Cabin after a long, jubilant campfire, Maya and I were ready to drop.

Maya yawned as she came out of the bathroom in her pj's. "I can't wait for the campers to get here," she said, "but I also wouldn't mind about fifteen hours to sleep before they do! I'm beat."

I smiled. "I'm sure it'll be fine, Maya," I said, smoothing my own pj's and fluffing my pillow. (I'd selected the bottom bunk this time, after my desperate pee dreams the night before.) "You were an *amazing* help today. Thank you so much. I'm really glad you're here."

Maya's face lit up in her now-familiar contagious smile. "Thanks, Nancy. I'm glad I was assigned to your bunk. This is going to be great!"

We turned off the lights and climbed into our sleeping bags. I think I was basically asleep before my head hit the pillow. But not for long. It couldn't have been more than ten or fifteen minutes before I was awoken by a light tap, tap, tapping.

At first a woodpecker appeared in my dream about a football game . . . which made no sense, and I guess was just my brain's last-ditch attempt to keep me from waking up. But eventually my eyes cracked open and I groaned.

"What is that?" I asked out loud.

Maya was stirring in her bunk above me too. "It won't stop! It sounds like it's coming from the window."

I turned. On the wall behind our heads was a small, screened window. Normally it would be open, but we'd closed it before going to bed because the night air was a little chilly.

It took a moment to make out the shape in the dark, but when I did, I gasped: a fist was knocking on our window!

"Who's there?" I demanded.

A pale face appeared in the window. Maya and I both gasped, but as the shock faded, the features started to look familiar. . . .

"Bella!" I cried.

"Shhhh, do you want to get caught?!" Bella glared at me. "Open the door, Nancy! We're all sneaking down to the lake!"

"Who's 'we'?" I asked, but Bella's face had already disappeared, and I heard footsteps pattering around to the door of the cabin. From the sound of it, Bella had already recruited quite a few other counselors.

I looked up at Maya, who was peeking over the side of her bunk. "They're sneaking down to the lake?" she whispered. "That sounds like fun."

"I thought you were tired," I whispered back.

She scrunched up her face. "I *am*," she said, "but I don't want to miss anything."

I sighed. Maya's words captured my feelings perfectly. I was really not in the mood to sneak around in the woods with Bella, of all people. But what if they all started having fun without me?

I scooched out of my sleeping bag and swung my legs to the floor. A loud tapping sound was already coming from the cabin door. "Hurry up!" a voice hissed.

I stumbled over to the door and swung it open. Nine faces greeted me: Charla, Maddie, Frankie, Bella, Susie . . . and George, Marcie, Bess, and Janie!

"George? Bess?" I asked, looking at them in surprise. "You're part of this?"

Bess looked sheepish, and George replied, "I know. I just didn't want to miss—I mean, make Marcie miss anything."

Marcie nodded solemnly, patting the notebook she'd slid into her waistband.

Maya walked up behind me. Bella looked us up and down.

"Get some shorts on," she hissed. "We're all going down to the lake to get to know one another!"

I wondered what Bella had in mind—some kind of nightlong version of Truth or Dare? I *hated* Truth or Dare. But the group was already walking over to the path to the lake, like they were just assuming we would follow.

I turned to ask Maya what she thought, but she suddenly jumped in front of me, her pj pants replaced by sweatpants. She was pulling on a pair of flip-flops. "Come on, Nancy!" she said, her face full of excitement. "We don't want them to leave without us!"

I hesitated for a moment. This was *clearly* against the camp rules—and we needed our sleep! But then, I reminded myself, wasn't this what camp was *really* about? Not just sports and crafts and whatever—but really getting to know your campmates?

"All right," I said, pulling open a drawer from the dresser where I'd unpacked my stuff. "But if it's Truth or Dare, I'm coming back here to sleep!"

The breeze off the lake was chilly, and I'd forgotten to bring a jacket. Still, I hugged my arms around myself to keep warm and kept smiling at Maya, who looked like she'd found a winning lottery ticket.

"This is what I used to daydream about when I wondered what camp might be like!" she whispered to me as we walked. "Sneaking out at night in my pj's, telling secrets . . ."

I nodded. When Maya put it that way, it *did* sound like a lot of fun. *Maybe I just need to loosen up and enjoy myself,* I thought. We'd been so busy over the last couple of days, there really hadn't been a lot of time for "bonding," as Bess would call it. And I barely knew the CITs, besides Maya, at all. It *would* be nice to have a chance to just talk.

Bella led the way down the path toward the lake and stopped when we got to the narrow, sandy beach that led down to the pier. It was where I'd had my crazy swim test the day before, and I shivered a little—whether from the memory or the cold, I couldn't tell. There were tire tracks cutting through the sand, from the company that had come to rip out the reeds today, I guessed. *Maybe that will fix the problem.* I hoped so, and tried to erase the memory of the dark figure from my mind.

Bella turned and faced us all. "Let's have a seat, shall we?" she asked, settling down in the sand. Everyone followed her lead, and we arranged ourselves in a tight circle. The sand was cool and felt damp on my legs. I looked up at the sky.

"Look at the stars!" I cried. A couple of people laughed at my enthusiasm, and I felt a little silly. But it really was amazing how clear the stars were out here, miles and miles from the nearest city. I could make out several constellations. The moon shone brightly too, pale silvery white and nearly full.

"It's really pretty," Maya said quietly, and a few others agreed.

"I live in Chicago," Frankie shared. "We almost never see this many stars."

Bella looked up. "It *is* nice," she agreed. "You know, I brought a flashlight we could use to see, but maybe it's nicer like this. We can just enjoy the moonlight."

"Where is everybody from?" Charla asked suddenly. "I know most of the counselors, and we just found out that Frankie's from Chicago, but where are the rest of you guys from?"

We all went around and talked about where we lived. Bess, George, and I shared a turn, talking about River Heights.

"Sounds like suburbia," Bella put in, not terribly kindly. "Do you live at the mall?"

"Yuck," George replied. "Do we have a mall? Yeah. Do I set foot in it more than once a year? No. Do I always regret it when I *do* go? Oh yeah."

"That's 'cause you always try to go around the holidays," Bess sniffed, then smiled to show she was kidding. "Rookie mistake."

"I'm kind of from suburbia too," Janie put in. "Statistically, probably most of us are."

"Not me," said Maya. "I live about an hour from here, and my town has, like, two hundred people in it. There are probably more cows than people!"

"Wow! How big is your school?" Frankie asked. "Is it super tiny?"

"My town doesn't have its own school system. We ride the bus to the county school," Maya explained. "But it's still really small!"

After a few more minutes of chatting and getting to know one another, we were startled by a loud throat clearing from Bella.

"This is all super exciting," she said, with a wolfish look, "but why don't we get down to the program?"

Bess pushed her hair behind her ear, frowning. "What *is* the program?" she asked. "I thought this was why we came. Just to get to know one another."

Bella shrugged. "Like I said, that's *super* exciting," she said, and I couldn't tell whether she was being sarcastic, "but I had something else in mind."

She reached behind her and pulled out a tote bag that I hadn't even noticed her carrying when we'd walked to the beach, which was unlike me. (I glanced surreptitiously at Marcie—Mini-Nancy—wondering if she'd caught it and written it down in her notebook.) Bella reached inside and pulled out a few items. As she spread them on the beach and the moonlight hit them, I noticed a white pillar candle, matches, and . . .

"Is that what I think it is?" Charla asked, scooting back. "I don't want any part of any—"

Bella's eyes flashed. "It's a *Ouija board!*" she said excitedly. "Has anyone used one before?"

Slowly, Maya raised her hand. Susie and Maddie followed suit.

George snorted next to me, and when I looked at her, I realized she looked totally disgusted. "Bella, you're not planning some kind of . . ."

But at the same time, Bella blurted out, "I thought we could have a séance!"

A séance? As in, a ritual to communicate with the dead? Automatically looking to Bess and George, I could see they thought this was as bad an idea as I did.

"A séance for who?" Janie asked, looking back and forth between Bella and George. "No offense, but . . . why would we have a séance here?"

Bess abruptly stood. "No reason," she said, glaring at Bella. "Let's go, Janie. We should really get some sleep."

But Janie was still looking to Bella, whose mouth dropped open in dramatic shock. "You haven't told her?" Bella asked.

"Told me what?" asked Janie, her frown growing as she looked around the circle.

"Nothing," George said, standing too. "There's nothing to tell. Just some dumb ghost story that Bella made up."

Bella scowled. "You *wish* I made it up, George," she said, picking up the matchbook. "You guys, why would I make up a story like that? You remember I'm from around here, right? And *Maddie knows it too.* Right, Mad?"

George let out a sigh as Maddie looked uncomfortably at her feet.

"I told you I've heard something like that, yeah," she said. "That doesn't mean I know it's true, but . . ."

"Know *what's* true?" Marcie suddenly cut in. "You guys, come on. We're not *babies*. Whatever this story is, you can tell us."

Bess, realizing that no one else was about to leave right now, groaned and sat down again. So did George, but she didn't look happy about it either. I shifted uncomfortably in the sand as Maya shot me a curious look. *You'll see,* I mouthed.

Bella grinned smugly, sitting up straight. "It's about Camp Larksong," she said. "The real reason why it closed."

Maya furrowed her eyebrows. "I thought they just ran out of money or something," she said. "I mean, I assumed."

"No," said Bella. "That wasn't why. Something *happened* here."

She let those words hang in the air for a moment.

"Right by this lake, in fact," she added after a few seconds of silence. "It happened during the big end-of-camp campout. You Camp Larksong people, you must remember it. Everyone cooks dinner over the fire and then sleeps in tents on Hemlock Hill. . . ."

"I remember," Maya said, her voice tense. "What happened?"

"Well, one year," Bella said, "the last year the camp was open . . . The rumor is, one of the counselors went nuts. She was having mental health issues or something, but nobody knew. And she kind of lost it during the middle of the night of the campout."

"I'm pretty sure that's not how mental illness works," George muttered, but her voice was so low, nobody seemed to hear her.

"She took one of her campers down to the lake," Bella went on, "and convinced her to go swimming. Then, after kind of frolicking around with her for a few minutes, she suddenly grabbed her by the hair and held her under." Bella shook her head, like she couldn't believe it herself. "They say the camper had really long hair. The counselor just grabbed a hank of it and . . ." Bella mimed grabbing a bunch of hair in her fist, then slamming it downward. The motion was so violent, we all jumped.

Bess cleared her throat. "That, um, that story had a lot more details than it did the last time you told it," she pointed out.

Bella's eyes cut over to Bess. "What does *that* mean?"

"She means you could be adding details," George said. "Because you're making it up. Guys, seriously . . ." She looked around at the CITs, who all looked frozen in shock. "She's making it up. There was no news coverage of this story, ever." Bess suddenly cleared her throat, and George glanced at her. "No news coverage of *a counselor drowning a kid*," George added. "Which there totally would be, if a *murder* was committed at this camp."

"Unless they were trying to cover it up," a voice suddenly piped up from the circle. We all turned, with surprise, to Maddie.

"I just think it sort of makes sense there'd be no stories out there," she said with an embarrassed shrug.

"If Deborah and Miles paid a lot of money to buy this camp and restore it . . . I wouldn't want that information out there either."

George shook her head. "Okay, but . . . Deborah and Miles don't control the media," she said. "Do you really think you can just snap your fingers and remove a news story from the Internet? It's, like . . ."

"Impossible," Janie finished for her.

George shot her a grateful look. "Thank you, Min—I mean, Janie."

Bella shifted in the sand and put her hands on her hips. "We're spending a lot of time talking about this, but we're not proving anything," she said. "The fact is, there are all kinds of rumors in Potterville that this camp is haunted. And at least one of us has seen the ghost."

I startled as she turned her gaze on me.

"G-ghost?" I sputtered. "Hold on there. That's kind of an overstatement."

Bella rolled her eyes, then went on in an absurdly patient tone, like she was dealing with a moron. "What *did* you see, then?" she asked, turning back quickly to the others to explain. "Nancy was pulled under the water during swim tests yesterday. She could have *drowned*." She then turned back to me, looking expectant.

I sighed. "I thought I saw a figure," I said. "But I never said *ghost*. The truth is, I don't—"

"So, there you have it," Bella cut in, looking away from me and around the circle. "I think it's pretty clear there's *some* kind of spirit hanging around this camp, and *I* would argue, it's an unhappy one." She folded her arms in front of her. "*I* think if we held a séance, we might be able to talk to the spirit and, maybe, tell it to go away."

George snorted. "That's ridiculous," she said. "You just want to scare everyone! I don't know what your deal is, but you love the drama. These kids just got here," she said, gesturing around to the CITs, "and the last thing they need on their first night is to stay up until the wee hours scaring away a ghost that doesn't exist. Come on, Marcie. This is ridiculous."

Marcie looked slowly from Bella to George, then stood. She glanced nervously at Bella. "I think your story *is* a little far-fetched," she said. "No offense."

Bella pursed her lips. "Whatever, ginger," she said snarkily. "Be on your way, then."

Bess gently tapped Janie's shoulder too. "Let's go," she said urgently. "I don't want to get in trouble. And I think this is silly."

Janie nodded. "Okay," she said, then turned and followed Bess back toward the path.

I slowly got to my feet. "I'm leaving too," I said, and then suddenly remembered Maya and touched her arm. "I mean, I think we should leave."

Maya looked up at me then, and I saw that her face was pale. "Yeah," she said simply, standing up.

"Do what you want," Bella said, shrugging. "I know Maddie wants to stay here. And Charla—don't you want to know the truth?"

"I'll stay," Maddie said quietly, not looking at anyone.

Charla just sat very still, looking thoughtful.

I glanced over at George, who lingered at the edge of the path where Bess had disappeared a moment before. She still looked upset, and I thought I knew why.

"Here's the thing," I said, reaching down to grab the candle and the Ouija board. "I'm not coming to your séance, Bella, and if you go ahead with it, I'm going to wake up Deborah and Miles and tell them."

"*What?*" Bella asked, scowling. "Who died and made you camp police, Nancy?" She leaned toward me, like she was going to grab for the candle.

"Nobody," I said, clutching the candle harder as I gestured around the circle at the CITs. "But these kids just got here. They're here to help us, but it's also our responsibility to take care of them. And tomorrow, busloads of kids are going to pull into the driveway, and it'll be our responsibility to take care of them, too."

Bella glared at me. "I *know* that. Unlike you, remember, I've been to camp before."

"You need to let go of this ghost story," I went on, trying to keep my voice even and low. "It's not helping anybody, and you could seriously scare some of the kids. I don't know what your deal is yet, exactly, but I don't even think *you* believe it."

Bella kept glaring at me. Her eyes looked hard in the pale moonlight. "You don't know what I believe," she hissed finally.

"Let it go, Bella," George said, raising her voice to be heard from the path. "Everyone, come back to bed with us now. Or Nancy and I will wake up Deborah."

One by one, the remaining counselors and CITs began getting to their feet. Several of them looked relieved. Maddie still avoided my eyes and looked a little embarrassed. But her CIT, Frankie, eagerly strode toward the path. Bella was the last to stand, and when she did she moved very slowly, deliberately grabbing her bag and tossing the matchbook, which was still in her hand, inside.

She took the few steps over to me, looking me right

in the eye. "I'll take the candle and Ouija board back, please," she said icily.

"I think I'll hold on to them," I said, not backing down.

A flash of anger played across Bella's face, and then her eyes hardened even more. She leaned in and whispered to me, "You're a goody-goody and a tattletale. I thought this camp would be *fun,* but not with squares like you and your little nerdfighters screwing things up." She held up one finger, and while I stared at it, wondering what she would do, she suddenly moved forward and poked me in the nose. "Were you looking to make an enemy tonight? 'Cause you've got one."

She backed up then, raising her voice so everyone else could hear, and pasted on a fake smile. "All right, séance postponed! Let's all get some sleep, people."

She strutted up the path as though she were still in charge. Slowly, we all fell into step behind her.

"Nice job, Steely-Eyed Nance," George whispered,

nudging me with her elbow. "You told her who was boss."

"But I definitely made an enemy," I added, shooting George a concerned look. "I just hope it doesn't come back to bite us later."

CHAPTER FIVE

~❦~

Making Friends

"NANCY!" SAM SAID BRIGHTLY, HER BASEBALL-capped head popping up in the open door of Juniper Cabin, "I've got another one for you! This is Kiki."

Sam backed away and a bright-eyed, smiling face appeared in the doorway, her braided hair held back by a colorful headband. "Hi! Is this my bunk?"

It was nine thirty the next morning, and I felt like it should be about five o'clock in the afternoon. Whole lifetimes seemed to have passed since breakfast! Four of my six expected campers were already milling around the cabin, chatting eagerly, choosing bunks, unpacking their things. Maya and I helped as much as we could and tried to keep the conversation going, not that the girls needed much help in that area.

"It sure is!" I said, jumping in front of Kiki with a smile. *Ugh, I'm so sweaty! Too much running around in too short of a time!* "Welcome, Kiki! It's so nice to meet you. I'm Nancy, your counselor, and this is Maya, your CIT. We're going to have so much fun this week!"

Kiki grinned. "Awesome!" she said. She looked around the room and her face fell. "It's just, I need a top bunk. I *hate* the idea of being boxed in. And is there a place I can plug in my phone?"

"Um, how did you talk them into letting you keep your phone?" I asked. Phones were not allowed at camp. Not that we had any service out here, anyway.

"I just pointed out to them that it doesn't *work*," Kiki said. "So I can't really use it. But I just like to have it with me. It's like a security blanket, plus my camera. And I intend to take a bunch of pictures and post them to Instagram as soon as I get back to civilization! No offense," she added quickly, reaching out to touch my shoulder.

It took me a minute to figure out what she meant. "Uh, none taken," I said. "I don't live here either, remember?"

"Right, right," said Kiki, looking around at the girls milling all around us. "HEY, LADIES! Would anyone be a super sweetheart and trade me for a top bunk? I would *totally* pay you back with a pedicure. I do the best nail art, not to brag!"

The other girls all circled around Kiki, peppering her with questions as Cece, a camper from Chicago, cheerfully led her to her top bunk. I looked at Maya and slowly shook my head, impressed. The campers had such confidence so far! I couldn't imagine walking into a cabin full of strangers like that and commanding the room—but it was a nice quality to have.

Maya moved closer. "Just one more," she whispered.

"That's right." I glanced out the door again but didn't see anyone heading in the direction of our cabin. Outside was total pandemonium. Campers climbed off buses, which had brought them from bigger cities like Chicago, or emerged from cars, surrounded by concerned parents and siblings. They met Deborah or Miles, who looked up their assignments on their clipboards and then passed them on to Sam or Taylor to bring to their correct bunks. The next hour had been reserved for a "getting to know you/unpacking" period, followed by a special hike and picnic lunch, led by each bunk's counselor and CIT. Maya and I had already looked over the camp map and planned a long hike to Mushroom Creek, way on the north border of the camp property.

"How are you holding up?" I whispered to Maya. When we'd returned from the lake the night before, it had been clear to me that Maya was scared by all the ghost talk. She wouldn't admit it, but she seemed pale and edgy, not her normal bubbly, excited self. We'd talked it over a little, and I'd explained to her again that I strongly felt that the story was not true. I tried to downplay my own incident in the lake too, repeating that I wasn't sure what I had seen. But Maya still seemed a little nervous. She'd tossed and turned for a while before finally falling asleep.

I shouldn't have listened to Bella and gone to the stupid lake in the first place, I chastised myself now. *Oh well. Next time I'll know.*

Maya shrugged. "I'm okay. Everything seems different in the light of day."

I knew how she felt. Even though the past two nights had been filled with creepy, ice-cube-down-the-spine moments, it was hard to recall those feelings when the sun first shone into our cabin. Even more so now, when our cabin was full of giggling, smiling campers.

A light knock on the cabin door turned my attention away. It was Taylor, smiling eagerly. "Last one, right?" she asked, holding up a clipboard.

I nodded but looked around Taylor for the camper. Where was she?

Then Taylor gently said, "Go ahead—don't be nervous!" and nudged a small, blond-ponytailed girl into the doorway. She hugged a dark-green backpack and had large, tortoiseshell-frame glasses.

"Hi," I said warmly, sensing that she might be shy. "I'm Nancy, your counselor. Welcome!"

The girl just nodded and looked at the floor.

"What's your name, honey?" Taylor prodded her.

"Harper," the girl whispered, without looking up.

I glanced at Taylor. *Okay—so she's going to be a little bit of a challenge.* "Come on in, Harper," I said, moving closer and taking her backpack from her. "Whoa—what's in here? It weighs a ton!" I added, smiling.

She glanced up shyly. "It's full of books," she said. "My parents said I shouldn't bring them all, but I didn't want to leave them behind."

"I like books too," I said, leading her into the cabin. "I think you're our final camper to arrive. Which means you'll be bunking here, with . . ." I put Harper's heavy bag down on a bottom bunk and looked at the girls, who stood around, watching us with openly curious looks. "Kiki?"

Kiki tossed her hair and walked forward confidently, holding out her hand as if to shake. "Hi there, I'm Kiki Pendleton," she said. "Who are you? Where are you from? Do you wear the glasses all the time? They're kind of cool. Are you from the city?"

Harper glanced from Kiki to me, then seemed to shrink into herself a little. She looked down at the floor and said softly, "Harper. Um, excuse me."

She walked around me to reach her bag and carefully unzipped it, pulling out a thick blue book with pictures of dragons on the cover. Then she pulled out another book, this one green, but clearly from the same series, with the same dragons zooming around the jacket.

A frown played across Kiki's face, and she looked from me to the other girls, who still stood in a cluster around her. "Um . . . cool. You must like books, huh? So where are you from?"

Harper lifted two more books out of her bag and then piled them all into a stack. She carefully lifted them and carried them around the bed to the dresser at the end.

"Um, I put my stuff in the three bottom drawers there," Kiki said. "There's only four dressers for eight people, so we'll have to share. There's some closets near the bathroom, though. Is that okay?"

Harper didn't even look up. She hefted the books on top of the dresser. Then she shrugged—the only sign she'd heard Kiki—and began carefully arranging the books, lining them up along the dresser's top edge. When she had them carefully placed, she tapped her lip and then switched the two on the outer edges. Then she nodded to herself, went back to her bunk, and began pulling out her clothes.

Kiki looked a little taken aback. I could tell she was trying to be friendly, but she seemed to have reached the end of her patience. "Oookay," she said quietly. "I guess we'll get to know each other later. Um, anyway"—she turned back to the others—"have you guys ever seen that show *Camp Confessional*? It's, like, my *favorite*!"

"Oh yeah!" one of the other campers, Winnie, cried. Winnie was Asian, with gorgeous glossy black braids, and had arrived with a curly-haired brunette named Katie. The two seemed to be BFFs. "Katie and I, like, totally binge-watched that on Netflix last weekend! We wanted to prepare. This is our first time at summer camp."

As the girls chatted, Harper finished arranging her clothes in the dresser and carefully closed the top drawer. She folded her backpack with military precision and tucked it between the dresser and the wall.

I walked over to her. "Did you have a long drive to get here?" I asked. I knew it was a lame question, but I was desperate to get this girl talking.

Harper shrugged again.

"An hour? Less?" I prodded.

"About an hour." She twisted her lips to the side, then looked away from me, back at the line of books. "Is it okay if I read until lunch?"

I struggled not to look too disappointed. I knew we'd just met, but I *so* wanted this girl to open up! The other girls were already chattering away like they'd known one another their whole lives.

"This is, um, sort of a 'get to know you' hour," I said, gently putting a hand on Harper's back and guiding her over to the rest of the girls. "Girls, why don't we all have a seat on the beds and get to know one another? We have an hour before our hike and picnic lunch."

"Oh, cool!" cried Katie, twisting some curls behind her ear. "Can we play Truth or Dare?"

I cringed. "No," I said, "but we can definitely ask each other some get-to-know-you questions!"

Maya ran over, clutching a book and bouncing up and down on the balls of her feet. "Nancy, here's that book I told you about," she said, holding up a small paperback titled *100 Great Questions*. "Maybe we can use some of the questions in here, and go around the bunk?"

"That's a great idea," I said, smiling. Maya, who was a total extrovert, had told me the day before about a book she'd brought full of icebreaking questions to help the campers—and the two of us—get to know one another. I knew I was lucky to have such an enthusiastic CIT.

But as we all settled down on the bunks, I noticed that Harper sat cross-legged on the floor rather than sit on a bed close to Cece. And she wore a distant expression as we all chatted eagerly, like she'd rather be someplace else. When someone asked her a question directly, she answered politely but rarely used more than a few words. As soon as she'd finished speaking, she turned her attention back to the floor in front of her or out the window.

I could understand being a bit of an introvert. Crowds sometimes made me uncomfortable, and I always loved returning to the quiet of my room at the end of the day. But this seemed a little more extreme.

How am I going to draw Harper out of her shell?

"Are we there yet?" Cece asked for the twenty-seventh (or at least, that's how it felt) time, and the rest of the campers cracked up over what had become a running joke.

"Almost," I replied, just as I had every other time she'd asked the question so far. "But really this time. It's just"—I unfolded my map and stared at the upper right corner—"right over this hill."

"Didn't you say that half an hour ago?" Winnie whined.

Nina, a tall, skinny girl with freckles and short

blond hair, scoffed, "We've only been hiking for, like, forty minutes, guys. Toughen up!"

"Easy for you to say," Kiki said with a sigh. "You're, like, some kind of amazing basketball player or whatever. But I'm just a *regular girl*!"

"What does *that* mean?" Nina asked, frowning. "Athletes are regular girls too!"

I glanced at Maya and sighed. We'd been hiking longer than I'd thought we would—we might have been a little overambitious in choosing Mushroom Creek as our destination—and the girls were getting cranky. All the getting-to-know-you good vibes seemed to have dissipated, and the girls were focusing now on how much they *didn't* have in common.

"All I mean," said Kiki, turning to Nina with exaggerated patience, "is you're, like, *conditioned* to do this. At home, the most I walk is around the mall with my sister!"

Nina cocked an eyebrow. "Have you ever thought that might make *you* the abnormal one?" she asked. "Maybe you should get more hobbies."

Kiki whirled around, clearly ready to give Nina a piece of her mind. But before I could figure out what to say to defuse the situation, Katie suddenly pointed ahead of us and shouted.

"OMG, you guys!" We all turned in the direction she was pointing. "Is that the creek?"

I checked my map. *Oh, thank heavens, yes.* "It is!" I said happily. "See, I told you! We *were* almost there."

"Thank goodness," Cece said. "I'm hungry enough to eat my sneakers. I was too excited to eat much breakfast this morning."

"Me too," Winnie added.

"Me too," said Nina with a smile.

I glanced back at Harper, all the way in the back, but she remained silent, looking into the woods around us. She hadn't said a word the whole hike, except one "excuse me" when she bumped into Cece.

"So guys," I said when we'd reached the edge of the burbling creek, "let's spread out our blanket and settle down here. This looks like a good place for lunch."

"*Any* place would look like a good place for lunch

right now," Maya pointed out, holding out the bag that held our sandwiches. "Nancy, shall we lay everything out buffet-style and we can all serve ourselves?"

"Good plan," I agreed.

Once we had the food all laid out and had each grabbed a plate, everyone tore into their sandwiches and chips. Things grew silent for a few minutes, except for the babbling of the creek and the sound of chewing. Then, suddenly, Nina spoke up.

"Are we going to do everything together?" she asked, looking pensively into the water. "Like, our bunk? Or are we going to be in different groups for different activities?"

I paused and put down my sandwich. "We'll be together for most activities," I said, thinking. "You'll mix with some other bunks for some things, like swimming or sports. But for the most part, we'll all be together."

"Oh." Nina crumpled her sandwich wrapper in her hand, not looking entirely happy.

"Why are you asking?" asked Cece. She'd been

watching our exchange curiously, and now her voice held an edge of annoyance. "Are we not, like, what you were looking for in a bunk?"

I shook my head. "Let's not make assumptions, guys," I said. "Why do you ask, Nina? Did you want to mix more with the other bunks?"

Nina pursed her lips, fiddling with the balled-up sandwich wrapper in front of her. "Not *exactly*," she said. "I mean, you guys all seem nice. I just thought . . . well, this is a Best of All Worlds camp. So I guess I thought there would be a few more sporty people in my bunk."

Winnie put down her sandwich and tilted her head in Nina's direction. "How do you know *we're* not sporty?" she asked. "I happen to play tennis on, like, a competitive level."

Nina's eyes widened. "Really?" she asked.

Winnie nodded. "I don't talk about it a lot. It's just something I've always done," she said. She smiled. "I kind of stink at other sports, though," she added. "Just so you don't get your hopes up."

Nina chuckled.

"You *guys*," said Maya, waving her hands in front of her as she often did, "one of the best parts of coming to camp is getting to hang out with people you never would have met back home! When I was at Camp Larksong—you know, that's what this camp used to be called years ago—my best friend ended up being this girl named Lucy, who was super quiet and into drawing. At the end of camp she drew this amazing graphic novel about all the fun we'd had! We're still friends now, and I still have a copy of her book."

I shot Maya a grateful look. "That's right," I said. "My best friends are here at camp too—they're counselors, Bess and George. You'll meet them later, I'm sure. But anyway, we have *nothing* in common—except how much we like each other! You'll see. Being *alike* isn't what makes you friends. It's appreciating what makes you different."

The girls all seemed to respond to that, and soon they were chatting and exchanging questions about the different hobbies they'd each mentioned during the get-to-know-you session.

As we were munching on dessert, freshly baked chocolate chip cookies, Katie looked over at Harper, who'd remained mostly silent through much of the conversation. "Hey, Harper," she said, adjusting her position to face her quiet bunkmate. "You seem a little quiet, and that's cool. But can I ask you a question?"

Harper glanced up, looking surprised and even a little nervous. "Um—okay?"

"What are those books you brought?" Katie went on. "Because I love to read, and I really like dragons, but I've never seen those books before. Are they any good?"

Harper's eyes lit up. "They really are!" she said, with more enthusiasm than I'd heard from her the whole morning. "They're called the Dragon's Eye Chronicles, and you might not have heard of them because they're only published in Britain. My dad buys them for me when he goes to London for work."

Katie nodded. "That's cool!" she said. "Can I look at them when we get back to the cabin? The art looked pretty."

"Me too?" asked Cece, raising her hand like we were in class. "I just read my first fantasy book, *Seraphina*, and I thought it was way cool."

Harper's cheeks flushed pink. "Sure," she said, crumpling up her trash with a shrug. "I'd be happy to show you . . . just make sure your hands are clean."

As we gathered up our trash and started heading back to the cabin, all complaints about being tired seemed to dissolve into the air, and the girls chatted happily about their favorite books, their favorite activities—all the things that made them *different*. If the girls noticed that Harper was still a little quiet and standoffish, they didn't seem to care. They were talking like there were a million things to learn about one another and they couldn't wait to learn them all.

I fell into step beside Maya at the end of the line and shot her a wink. "Nice job there," I whispered. "You might be a natural for this CIT stuff, Maya. You totally defused that fight!"

She held up her hand so I could slap her five, and

I did. "Same to you," she said. "I think we're going to make a great team, Nancy."

I smiled as I followed Maya and the rest of the girls down the path to the main camp.

As nervous as I was this morning, I thought, *camp is really starting to feel like home.*

"So how's it going?" Bess whispered as she slid in between George and me. We were sitting on a log, getting ready for the first full-camp campfire of the week. George and I had just been catching up on what was going on in our bunks. To her surprise, George was *loving* working with the younger girls.

"Marcie is amazing," she'd told me. "It's like she has this inner voice that tells her what each girl really needs. And the kids are *soooo* sweet. You know what's crazy about seven-year-olds?"

"What?" I asked with a smile. I'd already told her about my bunk, and the rocky start we'd had, leading into a pretty solid current situation.

George shook her head. "They don't argue with

you!" she said. "They just . . . it's all on their sleeve. If they feel happy, they act happy. If they feel sad, they cry and need a hug. It's so *easy*! Man, if I could deal with only seven-year-olds for the rest of my life . . ."

"You'd probably go crazy," I filled in for her.

"Maybe. *Eventually*," George allowed. "But for a week? This is living, Nancy. *This* is my ideal camp situation."

Now George smiled as she turned to Bess. "I can't believe I'm saying this," she said, "but it's awesome."

Bess widened her eyes. "George?" She reached out and put a hand on her cousin's forehead. George groaned and dodged away.

"I know," she said, "embracing a bunch of seven-year-olds is maybe not *expected* for George Fayne. But it happened, and I'm not ashamed. I'm loving my bunk. How about you?" she asked Bess.

Bess tilted her head from side to side. "So far, so good," she said. "I love my campers. They're great. It is kind of a challenge, dealing with the whole group dynamic. Like, we had this whole battle today between the kids who are still *super* into *Frozen* and the ones who think *Frozen* is for babies."

"Who won?" I asked. "I hope it was the over-it ones, or you'll have to hear 'Let It Go,' like, two hundred times over the next six days."

Bess snorted. "Next six days?" she asked. "You're so out of touch, over there in ten-year-old land. I've heard it *five* hundred times today alone. Luckily, I like the song." She began belting out her own version, but George quickly shushed her.

"How about you, Nancy?" Bess asked. I gave her an edited version of my adventures with the girls that day. Bess nodded. "Sounds like you and Maya are really gelling," she said. "That's great."

"Yeah," I agreed, glancing over to where Maya was sitting over on the other side of the circle with some other CITs. She was laughing and gesticulating wildly, clearly having a great time. "She's terrific."

Just then Deborah stood up and rang a cowbell she was holding, calling the campfire to order. "Campers, welcome!" she called. "I'm so happy to have you all here. I know that most of the campers are too young to remember, but some of the counselors and CITs may recall that at Camp Larksong, we always used to light this torch to symbolize the beginning of camp. The torch will stay lit all week, until we put it out on the last morning."

She moved back so that we could all see a large, metal-based torch that sat up in a clear area several yards from the campfire.

"Miles, are we ready to light it?" Deborah asked. Miles moved out of the shadows, igniting a long butane lighter, the kind you would use to light a grill. Everyone grew quiet as he walked over to the torch.

Deborah closed her eyes and said, "With eager hearts and minds, we light this torch to symbolize all the good times, precious memories, and lifelong friends we will make over the next week at Camp Cedarbark. May this torch light our way to happiness!"

"May this torch light our way to happiness!" the campers—and counselors—repeated.

Miles touched the lighter to the torch, and it blazed into a huge flame. I gasped. It was surprising and beautiful. When I looked over at Bess, I saw that her eyes were wet. She glanced at me and gave me an embarrassed smile.

"Oh, shush," she whispered. "You know this camp means a lot to me."

I hope it'll mean a lot to me after this week too, I thought. For the first time since we'd arrived, I felt really grateful to Bess for convincing us to come to Camp Cedarbark.

As I was turning back to the fire, I caught a glimpse of Bella out of the corner of my eye. She was wiping her eye too, staring into the flame. And her cheeks were bright pink, like she'd just been running, or—crying?

I wondered what was going on with her.

The rest of the campfire passed in a haze of songs, games, and one "spooky" (but not really) story from Miles about a bear he claimed used to hang around "a camp just like this one!" It was more corny than scary, but still, the campers shrieked and giggled. I was glad they were having a good time.

By the time the campfire ended and it was time to lead my campers back to Juniper Cabin, I felt ready to drop. I clicked on the flashlight I'd brought and slowly trooped up the path back to the main camp. Juniper Cabin was completely dark. I noticed footprints on the dirt path leading up to the door but figured we must have made them earlier, when we'd stopped by the cabin before the campfire.

Inside, the campers flitted around, grabbing their own flashlights from their dressers and flicking them on.

"Who's first in the bathroom?" Kiki called. "We have three sinks and three stalls, people. Who wants first shift?"

"Me!" called Cece.

"Me!" called Katie.

But I noticed Nina standing in the middle of the room, shining her flashlight beam on each bunk. "Guys . . . ," she said.

I looked where she was gesturing. Something was missing, but what . . . ?

"Oh my gosh!" I shrieked as it hit me. Maya and all the campers turned to me in alarm.

"Guys!" I cried, pointing at the bare mattresses. "Our sleeping bags are gone! Somebody stole all our sleeping bags!"

CHAPTER SIX

❦

A Sleepless Night

"OH NO!"

"Are you kidding?"

"You *cannot* be serious right now. . . ."

The campers all let out cries of disbelief as I swept my flashlight beam over all the bunks in the cabin. But there was no mistaking it: not a single mattress held the sleeping bags that each camper had brought with them and laid out on the beds just that morning.

"Where are we going to sleep?" asked Maya, her usually cheerful expression crinkled up into a frown. "Nancy, do you think this is a prank?"

A prank. I remembered what Bella had said when she'd led us all outside to scare us the first night of training: *It was just a prank.* Bess had agreed that pranks seemed to be a normal part of life at camp. But would someone steal all our sleeping bags as part of a prank?

There was only one way to find out. "Maya, keep an eye on the bunk for a minute. . . . I'm going to check some things out."

Maya scarcely had time to reply with an "okay" before I'd turned around and walked back out of the cabin. *The footprints!* I shone my light down onto the dusty path leading into the cabin. There they were: They looked like Converse sneaker tracks—a pretty common shoe wherever lots of young people congregated. They led away from the main camp, I realized now—toward the path to the lake. *Could someone have . . . ?*

"Nancy! Did it happen to you guys too?"

A voice came from behind me, and I swung my flashlight around to see Maddie, who had the nine-year-old bunk, standing in the doorway of Acorn Cabin.

"Did what happen to us?" I asked. *Old sleuthing trick: never give away what's going on. Make them say it first.*

Maddie sighed and shook her head. "Our sleeping bags are all missing!" she said. "Do you think it's some kind of prank?"

"It happened to us too," I called, as another voice chimed in from the darkness:

"Me too! I mean, us too!"

It was George, I realized, and swung my flashlight around to find her at the doorway of *her* cabin.

"Who would do this?" George asked, frowning. "Is this, like, a normal camp thing? Because I have a bunkful of exhausted kids here."

I heard someone running across the grass and quickly zoomed my flashlight around to catch Bella, coming from her cabin. She looked upset. "Are you guys missing your sleeping bags?" she asked.

"Yeah," I said. "Do you know anything about it?"

Bella stopped short and glared at me. "Oh, because I pranked you once, I'm responsible for everything that goes wrong at camp this year? Thanks for the warning!"

I shook my head and tried to make my voice less accusatory. "I'm just *asking*," I said. "You've been to camp before. You know what the normal pranks are."

Bella sighed. "Well, this might be a normal prank if it happened to one bunk. But it looks like it happened to all of us."

"Who would steal every sleeping bag out of every bunk?" Maddie asked from close behind me, making me jump. She must have walked across the clearing while I was talking to George and Bella. "How would you even *do* it? I mean, you would have to make several trips."

"If you were working alone," George pointed out. She had walked over to join the group too. "Maybe it was several people working together."

"Or maybe it wasn't human at all," Bella muttered, looking off toward the lake.

We all fell silent, staring at her.

"*What?*" she asked. "It's not like we have an angry spirit on the loose here or anything."

"You'd better keep your voice down," George whispered fiercely. "If my campers hear a word of this . . ."

Bella shook her head. "We could have taken care of all this last night," she murmured sulkily. "If you'd just let me have my séance."

I frowned, but turned my face so she couldn't see. *Why is Bella so obsessed with her séance and the supposed ghost?* What did she know? It was all very weird.

"Guys, there are footprints right here," I said, shining my light on the Converse tracks. "And unless ghosts commonly wear Chuck Taylors, I think our suspect is fully human—and it looks like she took several trips toward the path."

"She *or he*," a familiar voice piped up behind George. I glanced over to see Bess joining our little disgruntled circle. "Let's not be sexist. We're all missing sleeping bags, I'm guessing?"

"Yup."

"Uh-huh."

We all nodded.

Bess sighed. "Well, great. This was a lovely welcome for all the campers. I went to Deborah and Miles's house and let them know what's happening. Deborah was already in her pj's, but she was going to throw on clothes and come over."

"We already found footprints," I said, shining my light on the Converse tracks again. "Let's follow them. Maybe if we hurry, we can catch the thief in action. Deborah will find us."

"Sounds like a plan," Bess agreed.

We followed the trail—trails, in some places—of footprints across the main camp and into the woods, down the path that led to the lake. The cool breeze off the water made me shiver as we got closer to the beach. While I was starting to believe I'd hallucinated the figure I'd seen—or at least, I really wanted to believe that—the beach still gave me the heebie-jeebies. I'd have to try not to show it when my campers had swimming.

"Oh no," Maddie moaned as we followed the tracks to the beach. "Please tell me they didn't . . ."

But they had. The tracks left off just before the water's edge . . .

. . . And a soggy pile of sleeping bags was visible just beyond the waist-deep water.

"What happened?" Deborah's voice suddenly came from the path, and when we turned, she sprang out of the woods and onto the beach, her feet clad in bedroom slippers. "Did you find them?"

"I'm afraid so," said George, gesturing at the sodden pile of nylon and fleece that bobbed up and down with each ripple in the lake.

Deborah looked at the lake and seemed to take in what had happened. "Oh *no*," she murmured, shaking her head as she stepped closer. "Who would have done this? Did anyone skip the campfire tonight?"

We were all silent. No one had *skipped* it, that I'd known of—all the counselors and campers were present and accounted for. But it had been dark, and everyone's attention had been focused on Deborah,

Miles, or whoever was leading the singing or story-telling. It wouldn't have been hard for someone to sneak away.

I remembered Bella's flushed cheeks. *Did she . . . ?* And then I thought of the other counselors who had also been missing when I'd been pulled under in the lake. Sam . . . or Taylor? Could one of them have snuck away from the campfire, too?

"Maybe it wasn't a person," Bella suddenly said. While her voice was quiet, it seemed to echo in the silence.

Deborah looked at her, nonplussed. "What does that mean?" she asked.

Bella shrugged, not meeting Deborah's eye. "Some*thing* in the lake just seems to be really angry," she said. "What with the thing that pulled you down into the water, the thing that pulled Nancy down, the figure she saw. Maybe something's going on that's bigger than just some kid playing a prank."

Bella looked Deborah in the eye then, and something washed over Deborah's face. Recognition, or anger, or some kind of unwelcome realization that I couldn't quite put my finger on. Deborah met Bella's stare with her own intense one, and then the moment was over. She looked out over the lake and sighed, like she was accepting something.

"Miles and I will remove the sleeping bags from the lake and have them all washed and dried," she said in a low voice. "But I'm afraid there's no way we can have them ready for the campers to sleep in tonight. I'm very sorry, but you'll all have to sleep on the mattresses provided, and bundle up in your clothes. Tell the campers they'll definitely get their bags back tomorrow."

I glanced at Bess and George. It wasn't a surprise that the sleeping bags wouldn't be returned tonight, really—I'd suspected as much once we'd found them in the lake. But I wasn't sure how our campers would take the news. And I was more concerned about Deborah's reaction.

"If anyone knows anything about how these bags got in the lake," Deborah went on, "I would ask you to please come and talk to me or Miles, so that we can prevent it from happening again. I understand that some pranking is normal at camp, but a prank on this scale is unacceptable. Got it? Good. Off to bed, everyone."

She folded her arms and stared into the lake, but it was clear that she wasn't going to say any more. I looked around at my fellow counselors, and slowly we made our way back to the path and toward our cabins.

Bess poked my arm as we walked along. "What do you think, Nancy?"

I was silent for a minute. I was trying really hard *not* to think about it. "I don't know anything you don't, Bess," I said finally.

Back at the cabins, we said our good nights quietly, then split up to head back to our respective bunks. I told my wide-eyed crew that the sleeping bags had been taken to the lake—"It looks like someone's messed-up idea of a prank"—and that we, sadly, would have to make do with the mattresses for now.

"Who would do it?" Cece asked, once we had the lights out and were all lying on our mattresses, trying to snuggle with sweatshirts and jeans. "Who would think that was funny?"

"I really don't know," I admitted, trying to quiet my overactive sleuthing brain.

It was a long time before I could get to sleep that night.

"Nancy," George whispered as she settled beside me on a bench on the edge of the sports field. "I bet you didn't get much sleep last night."

I kept looking ahead, watching my campers, who were having a soccer lesson with Sam. "I didn't," I agreed. "That mattress was kind of cold."

"That's not what I meant," George scoffed, "and you know it. BESS!" She called across the field to where Bess had wandered. "Bess's kids have wood crafts this morning," George explained to me. "They were going to make a picture frame or something? Mine are swimming. I kind of like having these little breaks."

Bess caught sight of us and jogged over. "Hey, guys," she said, sliding in next to me on the bench.

"Were you talking about the Great Sleeping Bag Heist?"

I cringed.

"We were," George said, glancing over at me. "Sort of, anyway. I was trying to get Nancy to tell us her theories."

Bess's eyes lit up. "Nancy has theories! Awesome!"

I cleared my throat. "*Actually*," I said, "I have no theories. I have no feelings about the sleeping bag situation whatsoever . . . except that I would like mine back. I hear they're passing them out, washed and dried, after lunch."

Bess furrowed her brows. "What?" she said. "You, Nancy Drew, have no feelings about a developing mystery?"

"It's not a *mystery*," I groaned. *Please, let it not be a mystery.*

George was giving me major side-eye. "You're kidding, right?" she asked. "This is a *classic* mystery. Weird things happen! More weird things happen! Stakes are raised! You guys, I got, like, five hours of sleep last night." She sighed. "I never realized how much I need my sleeping bag. I may be a little weird today."

"How would we tell?" Bess asked with a smirk.

George shoved her.

"Someone stole some sleeping bags as a prank," I said, trying to ignore the feeling that I was attempting to convince myself. "That's all."

George shook her head. "Are you *serious* right now?" she asked. "You're forgetting how someone tried to *drown* you in the lake. Or the headlines I found about some tragedy happening here, and then Bella's weird story about the drowning."

I looked up at her, surprised.

"I'm not saying I *believe* Bella's story," she said, holding up her hands as though to wave off the idea. "I'm just saying, Google result *and* creepy ghost legend? *Something* is going on here. Where there's smoke, there's fire."

I was quiet for a moment. I wished what George was saying didn't make so much sense.

"What if this is all that happens?" I asked in a small

voice. "The sleeping bags disappear, and that's the last weird thing. Nobody getting pulled underwater. No weird sounds drifting over the lake."

Bess raised her eyebrows at me. "Do you really think that's likely, Nancy?"

I sighed. *No. Obviously no. Because that never happens when I'm around.* "I was going to take the summer off," I said plaintively, and it came out sounding like a whine.

"Evil never takes the summer off," George said resolutely, watching the soccer lesson.

I closed my eyes and rubbed my temples. *The summer was going so well so far. No missing pets, no weird threatening notes . . .*

"Oh look! It's Miles! I bet he could answer some questions for us! *Miles!*" cried Bess. I opened my eyes to see her jumping up and waving over the camp's codirector. He looked a little surprised, but walked up to us with a polite smile.

"Hello," he said. "It's George, Marcie, and Beth, I think?"

"George, Nancy, and Bess," Bess corrected him cheerfully. "I'm actually a Camp Larksong alum, and when I heard you were reopening, I convinced my two best friends to come with me this summer and be counselors."

"Oh, that's great," Miles said, fingering his scruffy beard. "Yes, Deborah always talks about how important Camp Larksong was to her. How much fun she had those summers."

Bess kept up the conversation for a few minutes, talking about her favorite Camp Larksong traditions and asking Miles how much he knew about them. Finally, just as I was beginning to wonder where all this was going, Bess tilted her head quizzically.

"The only thing I never understood," she said, "is why Camp Larksong closed so suddenly. It always seemed like the camp was doing so well."

Miles nodded, suddenly looking a little uncomfortable. "Well, yes," he agreed. "Yes, it was—"

"I heard vague things," Bess went on, "you know, from pen pals and things, after the camp closed. . . . I heard there was some kind of *tragedy* that happened here."

Miles grew quiet. He looked behind him, almost as if he expected to see Deborah there, ready to give him direction.

"Well," he said. "Well."

"I even found an old article," Bess said, "in a Google search just the other day, about a 'tragedy' happening here. And I thought, that's crazy, that we never heard about it! I mean . . . how *tragic* could it have been?"

Miles cleared his throat. "Well," he said again. "It was . . . It was unfortunate, yeah."

"What exactly happened?" George jumped in, unable to hide her curiosity any longer.

"Yeah," Bess said, "was it something to do with the lake? I heard it was something about the lake."

Miles sighed and looked around again, as though he were hoping to find someone to pull him out of this conversation. But when he saw no one, he hemmed and hawed a few times, then began:

"Well, okay, right, it was the last summer Camp Larksong was open. It was this week of camp, actually—the Best of All Worlds camp. Camp Larksong used to have one too, right?" He paused, and Bess nodded eagerly. "Right. Well, anyway, you know the last night of camp, there's always been the traditional campout on Hemlock Hill overlooking the lake. This one year, unbeknownst to her counselors or anyone else at the camp, one of the ten-year-old girls snuck out of her tent and went into the lake while everyone was sleeping." He coughed. "It was awhile before anyone heard her, and though one of the counselors jumped in and pulled her out, she nearly drowned."

I couldn't help looking at Bess and George with wide eyes. So . . . there *had* been a drowning? A near drowning?

"But she survived?" Bess asked, clearly confused.

Miles nodded. "I mean, it wasn't a great situation. She'd been without oxygen for a long time, and they were worried about brain damage. She was in the hospital for a while, I think. But she ended up okay."

I bit my lip. *So there was a near drowning . . . but no death.* That kind of cut Bella's ghost story up into a hundred little pieces. Living girls can't haunt. Living girls can't breathe under water long enough to drown someone else.

"It wasn't the camp's fault," Miles was saying, "but it hurt their reputation, you know? And I think it kind of broke the owners' hearts. So they closed it."

Bess took in a breath. "But—"

But she was cut off by a chorus of voices coming across the sports field.

"Nancy!"

"Nancy, check out my passing move!"

"Nancy, where's Maya?"

"Nancy, what time do we have to be at the mess hall for setup duty tonight?"

"I hate setup duty!"

"I know, but it's so much less gross than cleanup duty!"

I turned around to see my campers all barreling toward us across the field, pink-cheeked and excited.

Did forty-five minutes really go by that quickly?

I stood up. "You guys are done already?"

Kiki, who was in the lead, grinned at me. "Done? Not only are we done, Nancy, but Sam says I'm the most unique soccer player she's ever seen."

"I don't think that was a compliment," Nina muttered.

"What's next?" Cece asked brightly.

I glanced back at George and Bess. "Um, I think I'm going to have to take a rain check on the rest of this conversation!" I said with a smile. "It was nice talking to you, Miles."

George stood up. "I'd better go too," she said. "Bess's and my campers will be done any minute."

Miles nodded. "Nice talking to you girls too," he called. "See you later!"

All my campers circled around me as we walked back to the cabin for a quick rest before setup duty. They were full of funny, bubbly stories about one another and what had happened during soccer practice. Even Harper, who trailed behind the group with a dreamy expression, smiled when Cece explained how Kiki had yelped and jumped when she saw a bee.

I felt a rush of affection for these silly, innocent girls.

I have to do everything within my power to make sure they're safe, I thought. *Which means I'd better get to the bottom of what's happening at Camp Cedarbark.*

CHAPTER SEVEN

Something in the Lake

"NANCY, LOOK!"

I glanced up from where I lounged on a towel the next morning on the small beach on the lake. Harper leaped off the raft in a perfect swan dive, then reemerged a few yards away, beaming.

"That's amazing, Harper!" I yelled, clapping. That morning I'd been surprised to learn that Harper was, of all things, a super-talented swimmer. She said she'd been taking lessons since she was four.

Her eagerness to show off her skills wasn't always going down well with the other campers, though.

"Harper," Cece complained from her perch atop the raft as the quiet girl climbed up the ladder again. Her voice was loud enough to carry over the lake. "Can you please stop diving off every five minutes? Other people are trying to relax here."

Harper frowned at her. "I'm just doing what I like to do," she said. "And you're doing what you like to do. What's the problem?"

"The problem is you're getting me wet," Cece complained. "Every time you walk from the ladder to the other side to dive. And every time you do that, you send the raft shaking."

Harper glared at her. "You can't stop me," she said.

Cece groaned.

"Maybe you should get off the raft anyway," Harper suggested. "This is called *swim* period. Not lie-around period."

Cece glared. "Are you calling me lazy?"

"That's not what I said."

"Girls!" The lifeguard, a girl my age named Sandy, suddenly yelled from her chair on the pier. "Stop

fighting! Cece, Harper's right—it's time to get off the raft. Harper, move along."

Both girls let out huge sighs and gave each other one last angry look before Harper did another graceful swan dive, and Cece rolled her eyes and jumped off the side, feetfirst.

I lay back and closed my eyes for a few minutes after that. Swim period was one of my off periods— Sandy was supposed to be in charge. Which left me free to relax and daydream. I was writing a postcard to Ned in my head when suddenly a splash of water fell onto my nose.

"Hey!" I cried, opening my eyes.

"Oh, sorry," a soaking-wet Harper apologized, leaning over me. Water dripped down her wet hair and onto my towel. "I was just passing you on my way to the outhouse."

"Well, move along!" I said with a smile. "You're getting me all wet! Shoo!"

Harper chuckled and ran off. I closed my eyes again for a few minutes, trying to get back into my postcard, but I couldn't concentrate. Swim period would be over soon, anyway. So I sat up to watch the swimmers.

Just as I got settled in a cross-legged position, I heard a scream.

"Auuugh!"

And then there was a splash.

I jumped to my feet, turning my eyes in the direction of the all-too-familiar sounds. Kiki was treading water by the raft, looking horrified. "It's Cece!" she yelled to Sandy. "Something pulled her under!"

I felt my heart begin to race.

These girls weren't here for my swim test, I couldn't help thinking. *They don't know what happened. There's no way this could be a prank. . . .*

Sandy jumped up. "Stay where you are!" she yelled to Kiki, who was holding her nose in preparation to dive under and look for her friend. A stream of bubbles rose to the surface where Cece had disappeared. "I'll get her!"

In one fluid move, Sandy dove off the pier and slipped through the water toward Kiki. From where I stood on the beach, I lost sight of her under the dark, murky water. I found myself holding my breath as second after second passed with neither Sandy nor Cece reappearing. *What happens now?* I thought anxiously. *Do I go under and try to save them? I'm probably one of the weakest swimmers here. . . .*

But just as my heart felt like it might pound out of my chest, Sandy's blond head crested the surface, and she pushed Cece's head up above the waterline.

"Breathe," Sandy said. "Breathe. You're okay."

Cece was flailing, obviously panicked. But Sandy kept talking to her in a calm, reassuring voice. "You're all right. Just calm down so you can get the air in. In, and out. In, and out."

Slowly the panic left Cece's eyes and she began to breathe normally. Once she was breathing, Sandy helped her swim to the pier and climb out.

"Are you all right?" I cried, running down the pier to grab Cece by the hands.

Cece nodded. "I'm okay. It's just . . ." Her eyes teared up. "It felt like something *grabbed* me and pulled me down."

Sandy, who'd climbed out after Cece, frowned at me. "I heard there was some trouble with the plants at the bottom of the lake a few days ago. Maybe that was it?"

I took in a breath. *Sure, that's the official line—but plants can't grab you,* I thought. "Maybe," I said in a measured tone, and went back to comforting Cece.

After a few minutes, Cece came to sit with me on my towel and relax while swim period went on. Of course, I couldn't relax for anything now and sat ramrod straight on my towel, watching the girls. But after a little while, footsteps from the path attracted my attention.

I turned around.

Harper was emerging from the path. And she was still soaking wet.

My mouth dropped open, and even as I hated myself for having the thought, I couldn't help it.

Harper had been fighting with Cece.

Harper had disappeared a few minutes before the attack and reappeared a few minutes after.

Harper was a very, very strong swimmer—one who could, likely, hold her breath for a long time.

Even as the thought occurred to me, I shook my head in doubt. Harper was a *kid*, first of all. And she hadn't been at camp when whatever had pulled me and Deborah down had struck—unless that really *had* been reeds? And what was happening now was unrelated?

Harper barely paused as she walked past Cece and me on the beach. She didn't ask what Cece was doing out of the water. She just dropped her towel, barreled down the pier, and jumped in.

It was a few minutes before I realized how off my Harper theory was.

Because suddenly, with Harper paddling around just feet away, Nina started screaming.

"It has me! Something has my leg!" she screeched, before suddenly she was jerked downward and her head disappeared below water.

Cece and I both leaped to our feet. Sandy jumped up and dove into the water. I looked around, counting the other girls' heads in the lake, and was relieved to find them all accounted for, except Nina.

It was probably only seconds before Sandy and Nina reappeared, but it felt like hours. And when Nina resurfaced, she was still screaming.

"Auuuugh! It had me! Didn't you see it?"

"Calm down," Sandy insisted. "Nina, calm down and breathe. You're okay now."

"I'm not okay!" Nina insisted, shaking her head wildly. "Didn't you see it?! Sandy?" She sucked in a breath, then went on:

"It was human, Sandy. I could see its shape." She shuddered. "And its long, silvery-white hair."

This time Sandy pulled everyone out of the lake. Deborah was called. She appeared with her mouth drawn into a tight line, surveying the area like she was looking at a crime scene.

"All right," she said finally. "Juniper Cabin, I want you to move on to your next scheduled activity. I'm glad you're all okay. We'll talk about this later."

I shook my head. "Deborah," I said quietly, "I think the girls are kind of wound up. As am I," I added, with a nervous laugh.

She cut her eyes at me, no trace of humor in her expression. "And sitting around ruminating on it isn't going to calm them down at all," she insisted. "Take them to the crafts barn. Making something can be very relaxing."

Sandy raised her eyebrows at me. I opened my mouth to argue, but then stopped myself. Clearly Deborah wasn't going to budge. So I ran over to Maya, who'd spent swimming period writing letters home in the cabin, and asked her to take the girls to the cabin to change, then to the crafts barn while I spoke to Deborah.

"No problem," Maya said. Her usual cheery demeanor had been replaced by serious efficiency. "Catch up with us when you can, okay?" She led the girls down the path toward the cabins.

When they were gone, I turned back to Deborah. She was watching the lake with an unreadable expression.

Then, suddenly, she dropped her head into her hands and groaned.

"Deborah," I said, feeling like I was eavesdropping.

She lifted her head. "Nancy? Why aren't you with your bunk?"

I sighed, moving forward. "I asked Maya to look after them for a few minutes. I'm worried about what's going on at Camp Cedarbark," I said honestly.

Deborah shook her head dismissively. "It's not a ghost, if that's what you're getting at," she said, sounding a little annoyed.

"I know it's not a ghost," I said, adding silently, *Or at least I think it's not.* "But I saw a figure when I was pulled under the water too. What's going on?"

She pursed her lips and sighed. "The plants?" she said finally.

"I thought you had someone remove all the plants," Sandy said. She was standing on the other side of Deborah with her arms folded.

"She did," I agreed. "I thought the plants were removed the day the CITs arrived," I added.

Deborah shrugged. "Maybe there are still more? I don't know. *I don't know.*"

"Nina was quite insistent that she saw *a figure*," Sandy said.

Deborah sighed again, then rolled her eyes. "How would that work?" she asked. "Someone is holding their breath under there? Someone has gills?'

"I don't know. I'm just telling you what she said," Sandy retorted.

Deborah turned to her, softening her expression. "You're a lifeguard. If someone wanted to hang out under the water, not being seen by anyone, and pull someone down—is that possible?"

Sandy seemed to think for a moment, then bit her lip. "It is—well—*unlikely*," she murmured.

Deborah moaned again, rubbing her hand over her face. "We spent a lot of money on this camp," she said quietly. "I can't shut down the lake. I need this summer to be a success."

"Deborah, if there is a *figure* in the water pulling people down," I said, "it's probably the same person who stole all the sleeping bags and threw them in the lake. What if someone is trying to sabotage Camp Cedarbark? To keep you from being successful, for some reason?"

Deborah frowned at me. She looked honestly confused. "Why would someone do that?" she asked.

"I don't know," I said, "but I'm kind of an amateur detective, and I plan to find out."

CHAPTER EIGHT

~

The Secret File

THE NEXT MORNING WE WERE WOKEN UP to the sound of rain pouring down on the cabin's roof. Outside, the ground had been soaked to mud, and tiny lakes and rivers had formed all over the clearing in the middle of the cabins.

Cece groaned. "I was looking forward to the soccer game today," she said as she pulled a pair of jeans and a T-shirt out from her dresser.

"Maybe it will happen anyway, rain or shine," suggested Winnie.

"I don't think so," Maya replied, staring out the

window. "I think you'd need a pair of flippers to play in this! And maybe gills."

Gills made me think of what had happened at the lake yesterday, and a little shiver ran up my spine. As of today, I was officially on the case. And I meant to figure out who—or what—was responsible for first Deborah, then me and two of my campers being pulled underwater.

When we went to the mess hall for breakfast, Miles announced that after we were done eating, the campers would divide into two groups and spend the morning watching a DVD. My group, along with Bella's eleven-year-olds, would stay in the mess hall. The other kids would run next door to the crafts barn.

"Aw, man," Cece grumped.

"It's supposed to clear up this afternoon," I said, trying to sound cheerful. "Maybe we can fit the soccer game in then."

Cece looked dubious, but after a second or two she shrugged and finished her eggs.

Meanwhile, I was sensing an opportunity to get

some information. If everyone was going to be cooped up in the mess hall, that might give me a chance to talk to Deborah and Miles about everything they knew.

All I needed was a favor from another counselor. Unfortunately for me . . . the only group that was supposed to stay in the mess hall besides mine was Bella's.

I excused myself and strolled over to her table once I'd gobbled up my eggs and toast. "Hey, Bella," I said casually as I drew up behind her chair.

She turned, looked at me, and glared. "Oh, it's you," she said, clearly unimpressed. "One of the Perfect Triplets. Well, what's up? Have I violated the spirit of the camp somehow by wearing a not-cheerful-enough shirt?" She gestured down at her T-shirt, which was for some metal band called Eminent Distress.

"Um, no. I actually wanted to ask you a favor. I could pay you back any time."

Bella narrowed her eyes. "Why would I do *you* a favor?" she asked.

"Because we're both counselors?" I asked. "Because if you do, maybe I could watch your bunk sometime to give you a break? I mean, that might be nice."

Bella looked from me to her campers, who were all crowded around one girl's chair. The girl was holding up a letter she'd received and giggling. "Okay," she said. "I'm listening."

"I'd just need you to keep an eye on my bunk this morning," I said. "It shouldn't be hard. Maya will be there, and they're all just watching a DVD."

Bella frowned. "And what will you be doing while I watch them?" she asked.

"Research," I said tersely. When Bella kept staring at me and I didn't elaborate, she seemed to get the hint that I wasn't going to say more.

"All right," she said finally. "But you owe me!"

"Noted," I said before quickly spinning around and spotting Miles, who was setting up a movie screen in front of the stage. I darted away from Bella's table and walked briskly over to him.

"Miles," I said, and when he turned, looking

confused, I went on, "I was just wondering whether it's okay if Bella looks after my campers this morning. She says it's fine with her."

Miles raised his eyebrows. "While they watch the movie? Sure. But what will *you* be doing?"

"Weeeeeeell," I said, drawing out the word as I tilted my head, "I thought maybe I could talk to you and Deborah about what happened at the lake before Camp Larksong closed. Privately, of course," I added hastily.

Miles's expression changed suddenly, from mildly curious to completely closed off. "Oh," he said, turning back to the movie screen. "Deborah told me you're some kind of amateur detective. Is that right?"

"Yes," I said. "But mostly, I just want to help you guys get to the bottom of what's going on at this camp."

Miles turned back to me, wearing an expression of surprise. "What *is* going on at the camp?" he asked. "Besides some silly pranks and an issue with reeds in the lake?"

"I—well—" I stammered, wondering if Miles was

serious. "I thought you had the lake trimmed of reeds," I said. "And the girls who were pulled under—they said they saw a figure."

Miles snorted. "Including you, isn't that right?" he asked.

I nodded slowly, feeling like I'd been caught somehow. But I *had* seen a figure. . . . "Including me."

Miles turned away, fiddling with the screen again. "It's fine with me if you want to chat with Deborah," he said. "She's in the office. But I don't think I have any information that can help you. I'm not convinced there's a mystery to solve, Miss Nancy Drew."

I wasn't sure how to react. I'd gotten what I wanted—hadn't I? But why was Miles being so strange?

"Thanks," I said simply, and after saying a quick good-bye to Maya and my campers, I ducked out into the rain and ran across the clearing to the camp office.

It occurred to me as I ran how absent Miles had been from many of the camp activities. He always showed up for campfires, and was usually there for meals, but most of the day-to-day running-the-camp responsibilities seemed to be handled by Deborah. *She* was the one who had gone to Camp Larksong, I remembered. *She* presumably had wanted to buy the camp and reopen it.

Was it possible that Miles didn't want me looking into the "mystery" . . . because he had something to hide?

I pushed the thought from my mind as I knocked lightly on the screen door and then pushed it open. The camp office was on the lower floor of the modest two-story house on camp grounds where Deborah and Miles lived. When I walked in, Deborah was sitting at her desk, staring into a computer monitor. She looked a little surprised when she glanced up and saw me, but she soon gave me a little wave of welcome.

"Hi, Nancy," she said. "Where are your campers?"

"Bella's watching them for me," I replied. "You know, they're in the mess hall watching a DVD anyway. I thought maybe . . . Maybe this would be a good time for the two of us to talk more?"

Deborah took that in, looking at me with a

not-entirely-eager expression. "Okay," she said.

"I told Miles I could talk to both of you," I went on, "but he seemed sort of convinced that, um . . ."

"'There's no mystery to solve,'" Deborah filled in, making her voice deep and goofy—clearly her impression of Miles.

"Yeah," I agreed.

Deborah gave a little rueful smile and pushed her chair back from the desk. "It's not personal, Nancy," she said, giving me a kind look. "Miles is a pragmatic guy. He's not going to believe there's something going on unless it's *really* obvious."

A question suddenly occurred to me. "Do *you* think there's a mystery to solve?" I asked.

Deborah paused, looking thoughtful. "I think a lot of strange things have been happening," she said quietly. "Unsettling things. In a weird way, it would make me feel better if one person were behind them."

At least it's not just me, then. There was a chair on my side of the desk facing Deborah, and I sat down in it. "Can you tell me more about what happened that night in the lake at Camp Larksong?" I asked. "It seems like—for whatever reason—all the strange things that have happened seem to lead back to the lake."

Deborah nodded slowly, then wheeled her chair back and over to a large pine filing cabinet. She opened the top and began digging around inside. "Let me find the file," she murmured.

"You have a *file*?" I asked.

At that moment, Deborah pulled a manila folder from the cabinet and turned around, looking surprised at my question. "Of course I do," she said. "I wanted to know everything about Camp Larksong before we bought the land. There were all these rumors and . . ." She stopped and sighed. "I just wanted to be prepared."

She rolled her chair back over to the desk and pushed the file across the surface to me. I reached out and picked it up but didn't open it yet. "So what happened?" I asked. "What did you learn?"

Deborah cringed like I'd poked a bruise. "I didn't have to *learn*," she said after a few seconds. Then she closed her eyes and began speaking, like she was telling a story she'd already told several times. "It was strange because up till that night, it had been a perfect week at camp. The kids were really easy, and my bunk got along well. I had one girl, Lila, who was homesick and could be a little quiet and intense. But the other girls really liked her, and they all clicked as a group."

I rested my palm on the top of the folder, trying to follow what Deborah was telling me. My *bunk got along well?* Wait—she had been there?

"We got to the campsite a little too early to start dinner, so we all hiked down the path to the lake and went for a swim," she said. "Lila had this ring she'd gotten from her parents for her birthday or something. It was pretty, a little flower with a pearl in the middle of it. She was really proud of it." Deborah stopped and rubbed her eyes. "While we were swimming, I don't know what happened exactly, but the ring slipped off her finger."

"She lost it?" I asked.

Deborah nodded. "We spent at least an hour with

everyone trying to find it. But you can imagine—fifty campers in a small space, a lake with reeds and sand on the bottom . . . It could have been *anywhere*. And with everyone swimming around looking for it, we could have buried it under more sand and reeds as we were trying to find it."

"Sure," I agreed.

"Anyway," Deborah went on, "finally we had to give up and start dinner. After dinner, while it was still light, me and one of the other counselors swam out and tried to find it again. But we didn't have any luck. We had the campfire, and Lila seemed like she was okay, she was over it. She was singing and telling stories with everyone. So when it was time to go back to our tent and go to sleep, I figured it was over."

I figured it was over. "Wait—you were her counselor?" I asked suddenly.

Deborah looked at me matter-of-factly. "Yes," she said. "You didn't know that?"

Bella's tale suddenly came back to me. *A counselor went crazy and* drowned *a camper!* Did Deborah know that, in the rumors and stories about what had happened, she'd been painted as the culprit? Was that why she felt she had to have a folder full of research on the incident?

"No," I said, shaking my head. "But I'm sorry to interrupt. Go on."

Deborah cocked an eyebrow at me, but then went back into her story. She looked uncomfortable now. "The next thing I knew," she said, her words slowing, "I was woken up by screaming. It was the middle of the night, and one of the other campers had woken up and noticed Lila was gone," she said. "They were all freaking out. They thought it was a bear! She'd been attacked by something! In all the commotion, it was a few minutes before we got out of the tent and I noticed the footprints leading down the path toward the lake. . . ." She stopped there.

"She'd gone to the lake?" I prodded gently.

Deborah nodded, her face tense. "When I got there, I could hear her struggling in the water." She paused. "I screamed. It was all I could think of to do. God, I didn't even jump in after her! It was another counselor I'd woken up with my screams. She jumped in and found Lila under the water. I thought she was dead." Deborah's voice broke on the word "dead." I reached out and put my hand on hers sympathetically. But Deborah pulled her hand away.

"She wasn't dead, of course," she went on after a few seconds. "One of the other counselors pumped the water out of her chest and got her breathing again. We called an ambulance, and she was rushed to the closest hospital." She took in a deep breath through her nose. "She must have gone back into the lake to find her ring," Deborah said finally. "She was in the hospital for a long time, I know that. She'd been without oxygen for too long. There were rumors of brain damage. But I heard she recovered."

"You heard?" I asked.

Deborah looked up at me. Something flashed in her eyes—annoyance or defensiveness, I couldn't tell which. "Her parents were pretty angry with the camp, and me specifically," she said. "They sued

Camp Larksong. That's what cost the previous owners all their money—they ended up settling with the family. Anyway, I couldn't exactly go to visit Lila. I've lived with the guilt of not waking up earlier every day of my life since it happened. But I couldn't tell her how sorry I was."

Silence enveloped the office. I stared down at the folder, taking all of that in. *It wasn't Deborah's fault—or was it?* I tried to imagine one of my campers sneaking out to the lake in the dead of night. Would I hear it? If I heard it, would I be able to jump in after her and save her life?

What would it feel like to see one of my campers dragged out of the lake, barely alive? Hauled off in an ambulance to be in the hospital for weeks?

I shook myself, trying to disperse the terrible feeling that came over me. I glanced at Deborah, who was staring out the window, pain in her eyes.

"It sounds really hard," I said finally. "I'm sorry."

Deborah nodded slightly. "Don't be sorry for me," she said quietly. "I'm sure it was much harder for Lila and her parents. But maybe you can understand why, the lake . . . the thought of anything else like that happening there . . ." She stopped and shook her head. "I know what people say around this town. I know they say the camp is haunted, that something even worse happened here. But it *didn't*."

She was quiet for just a few seconds. "If there *is* someone behind the strange things happening around camp," she said, "they *must* know about Lila. Or they know some version of the story."

I let out a breath and pulled the manila folder into my lap. Carefully, I arranged it right side up and opened the cover. Inside were newspaper articles, pieces printed off the Internet, legal documents. I leafed through them all until something stopped me dead in my tracks, sending spikes of ice up through my chest.

A photo accompanied one of the articles. I held it up for Deborah to see. "Is this Lila?" I asked.

Deborah looked at the photo and nodded. "That's her," she said. "Lila Houston. She was thirteen years old."

My hand shook as I turned the article back around and placed it back in the folder, faceup.

Lila Houston stared up at me from what must have been a school photo. She had round, dark eyes—*and long, silvery-blond hair.*

CHAPTER NINE

~

A New Suspect

"IT'S A COINCIDENCE," GEORGE WHISPERED that night at the campfire. We'd settled on a log far from the main action, and I'd used the time to update her and Bess on everything Deborah had told me. "It has to be . . . right?"

"It seems like kind of a big coincidence," Bess said. "A girl with silvery-blond hair nearly drowns in the lake . . . and a few years later, swimmers are attacked by a figure with silvery-blond hair?"

I nodded solemnly. It takes a lot to freak me out, and I'm usually not one to believe in ghost tales. But *this* was really weird. The only thing was . . .

"Lila isn't dead," George pointed out pragmatically, looking from Bess to me. "Is she?"

"No." I shook my head. "Deborah says she's alive and ended up without brain damage or anything. Or so she heard, anyway."

George held out her hands. "Ergo," she said, "Lila can't be haunting the camp. Because people who are *alive* cannot *haunt*."

I took in a breath, trying to think. We were all quiet for a minute. The sound of the campers' current tune—"Kumbaya"—drifted over to us.

Someone's crying, Kumbaya . . .

"What if she's *not* alive?" Bess asked suddenly. "It's not like Deborah ever saw her after the accident, right?"

"But her parents *sued the camp*," George pointed out. "They settled, but for a lot of money. I think they would have mentioned if their daughter died."

Bess held up her pointer finger. "Okay, so she

survived the near drowning. But it's been five years. Maybe she survived, only to die of some *totally* unrelated thing later. And then . . ."

". . . then naturally she comes back to haunt the camp where she *didn't* die?" George asked, frowning. "If she died of something else, wouldn't she haunt the thing that actually killed her?"

"Maybe the other thing was really *boring*," Bess retorted. "Like an allergy to bee stings or something. Would you want to waste your afterlife haunting a bee?"

"*Guys*," I said, "I think we're getting off topic here. And I have a confession to make. This afternoon, I called Lila's parents on the pay phone and asked for Lila, pretending to be a telemarketer."

Bess crinkled her brows. "Did you talk to her?" she asked.

"No," I admitted, "but I did confirm that Lila is alive and well and still lives here. I also got an earful about the Do Not Call registry. Anyway . . . let's assume Lila is alive and well, and not haunting the camp. That wouldn't stop someone who knows about the accident from using it to harass Deborah and Miles . . . would it?"

Bess and George both looked thoughtful.

"Who would do that?" asked Bess after a few seconds.

"I don't know," I said, "but that's what I intend to find out."

Soon the campfire broke up, and I got to my feet to collect my campers. Before I could make my way over to where they were sitting with Maya, someone grabbed my arm.

"You're *welcome*," Bella said, "for watching your kids earlier."

I turned around in surprise. Bella wore a scowl, and she looked from me to George and Bess like we were all something stinky she'd stepped in.

"Uh, thanks, Bella," I said after a brief pause. "I'm sorry, I thought I'd thanked you earlier."

"It's just ironic," Bella said, grabbing a lock of dark hair and twisting it around her finger, "that *you* guys think I'm the bad one, when you're sneaking around when you're supposed to be watching your kids, doing God knows what."

"I was talking to Deborah," I explained patiently, "but thanks for the feedback. And I never said you were *bad*, Bella, I just didn't think involving a bunch of fifteen-year-olds in some made-up séance was a good idea."

"It wasn't *made up*," Bella whispered fiercely. "You just don't want anyone to know the truth about this place."

"What truth is that?" I asked, curious now.

Bella rolled her eyes at me. "You *know* what truth," she replied snarkily. "That this place is *mad* haunted. Anyway, it's fine, Nancy. I don't need you, or your little clique." She looked past me to Bess and George, who had started collecting their own campers. "I have my own clique."

With those words, she turned on her heel and strode away.

Why is Bella so interested in this supposed haunting? I wondered again as I watched Bella walk back to her campers and lead them down the path back to the cabins. *She says she's a Camp Larksong alum. . . . Could she possibly have been there that night?*

I swallowed hard, letting my mind lead me on. *Could she have an ax to grind with Deborah?*

I walked over to my campers and greeted them, listening to their cheerful stories about the day, and their banter with one another. I put my arm around Harper, who was bringing up the rear and seemed to be off in her own little world. But in reality, my mind was spinning on its own, a million miles away.

Bella could have dived back into the lake after she went to get her hoodie the day of our swimming tests, I realized. *She could have snuck away from the campfire the night the sleeping bags went missing. But how would she have gotten away from her own bunk to come harass mine while we were swimming?*

There was the matter of the silvery-blond hair, too. If Bella was at camp the year Lila nearly drowned, she might know her hair color, or she could have seen a picture in the news. But would she go so far as to wear a wig underwater to freak everyone out?

"Nancy," Harper said suddenly, tugging on my sleeve, "you seem sad."

I looked down at her, startled. "I do?" I asked. "I'm sorry, Harper. I don't *feel* sad. I'm just trying to figure something out in my mind."

"Oh," she said, looking away. "Well, I hope you figure it out soon."

Me too, I thought, patting Harper on the back. *Me too, kid.*

I was at a campfire, and Bess and George were sitting across the fire on different logs, but I couldn't get to them. There was a terrible wailing in the woods, like a young girl crying. It went on and on. Then, suddenly, the smoke from the campfire grew tendrils that formed arms and legs and a horrible smoke-bearded face! The smoke creature lunged toward me, snagging me in its long, spindly arms. I screamed, but no sound came out, and nobody noticed. I felt panic welling up in my chest as it lifted me up, carrying me away from the campfire, into the woods, where the wailing was getting louder and louder. Just as I was finally able to get my voice out—and let out a real scream—the smoke monster suddenly tossed me in the air, and I was spinning through the darkness, falling and falling, until with a SPLASH I was submerged in the icy lake. . . .

"Nancy!" Something grabbed my arm and shook it, and I shot straight up in bed, the shock of the icy water still making my heart pound.

"*What?*" I cried, startled. "What is it? What?"

Kiki, who'd been shaking me awake, jumped back, startled.

"I'm sorry," I said, waving for her to come close again. "I was just having this awful dream. . . ."

"Nancy, you have to get up," she replied, all business. "The cabin is flooding!"

~

CHAPTER TEN

An Unexpected Clue

I SAT UP IN BED AND LOOKED DOWN, AND that was when I noticed the other girls, shouting and splashing through the foot or so of water that covered the floor. Maya opened the front door, and all at once the water level decreased as a stream of water escaped.

"Oh my gosh! What *happened*?" I asked, jumping down from my bed. I hit the floor with an icy *splash* and shrieked. The water was freezing!

"Someone turned on all the showers and sinks,"

Maya replied. She was soaking wet from the waist down. "Cece got up to use the bathroom, and she found it."

"Did someone turn everything off?" I asked, sloshing through the water to the bathroom.

"Yup," Winnie replied. "Maya did it. Then she came to wake all of us up, but you were sleeping pretty hard."

Sleeping pretty hard. I remembered my nightmare and sighed. Clearly the whole situation at Camp Cedarbark was stressing me out. And now this—was this one more weird event to add to the list?

"All right," I said, taking stock of the situation. All the girls in the bunk were up, standing before me in various states of soaking-ness. "Let's get out of the cabin, then. We need to tell Deborah what happened."

"We do?" asked Cece. "What if this was just a prank?"

"It's a pretty destructive prank," I replied. "Flooding the cabin could cause a lot of damage, not to mention that someone could have gotten hurt if they slipped or something. No, I think this is bigger than a prank." I paused, watching Harper carefully arrange all her books on Kiki's top bunk. "Harper? Come on. Your books will be okay."

Harper glanced at me, clearly not convinced. "I don't want them to fall into the water," she said. "They're first editions."

"They'll be fine," I said, suppressing a frustrated sigh. "Come on, guys. Let's get Deborah and start cleaning all this up."

I half expected to see a commotion when we got out of the cabin—water spilling out of the other cabin, other counselors and campers lining up in the clearing—but we were met with dead silence. It looked like this "prank" was aimed at Juniper Cabin. Could I have been the target?

I asked Maya to watch the girls while I went to wake up Deborah and Miles.

I pounded on their front door for a few minutes. Finally I heard noise inside, and Deborah appeared in a terry-cloth bathrobe over a cotton nightgown. I wasn't surprised to see her and not Miles.

"What's up?" she asked.

I explained what had happened, and Deborah's expression turned serious. "It only happened to your cabin?" she asked.

"Yes."

She let out a deep sigh. "Do you think it's related to the other things?"

I breathed in. "Yeah," I said. "I think someone has figured out that I'm onto them."

In the end, Sam the sports counselor was also woken up by the commotion and came over to help. It took all of us about an hour of mopping and pushing the water out the door to get the cabin dry enough to go back inside to sleep. In the morning, we were understandably a little cranky. Breakfast was quieter than usual, with us silently chewing our pancakes, many of us staring into space.

"Why would someone come after us?" Maya asked suddenly, her eyebrows raised in confusion. "Only us?"

I could tell that the prank had rattled my normally

optimistic CIT, but I didn't know how to comfort her. Who *would* target only us? Someone who knew I was getting closer. Maybe Bella? Or . . . Miles? But it was hard to imagine a grown man sneaking into our bunk to flood it. It just seemed . . . juvenile.

"We don't really know what it was, Maya," I said slowly, but I couldn't help looking across the mess hall to the eleven-year-olds' table, where Bella was laughing so hard she looked like she was snorting. "Don't worry. Will you guys excuse me a minute? I'm going to talk to Deborah."

I stood up and walked over to the table by the kitchen where Deborah was eating with Sam, Taylor, and Sandy. Deborah looked up as I approached. "Hi, Nancy," she said, pulling out the empty seat next to her. "Come sit down."

Sam looked up curiously. She was wearing her ever-present Yankees cap. "Oh, hey. Did your bunk all get back to sleep last night?"

I nodded. "Eventually," I said.

Deborah quickly shoveled her last bite of pancakes

into her mouth and touched my shoulder. "Can I speak to you privately for just a moment, Nancy?"

"Sure."

I waved at the other counselors and the lifeguard, then waited while Deborah bused her tray and led me out the front door to the main clearing.

She took a deep breath. "I'm having trouble with something."

"What's that?" I asked. There already seemed to be plenty of trouble at the camp. . . . Was something even stranger going on that I didn't know about?

Deborah looked pained. "The big end-of-camp campout is coming up," she said. "You know, it's supposed to be tomorrow night."

I did know the campout was coming . . . but it surprised even me that it was only a night away. Where had the time gone? I felt like my campers and I were still getting to know one another.

"Wow," I said, having a sense where she might be going with this. "And you're . . ."

"I'm scared something else will happen," Deborah

said plainly. "Up until last night, I could explain every-thing away as pranks gone wrong. The sleeping bags in the lake, some kid playing silly games in the water. But last night was different. It could have caused major damage to the property. And . . . with the water ele-ment, it *does* all seem to lead back to the lake, and what happened to Lila."

I nodded slowly. "And what happened to her hap-pened at the campout," I filled in.

"Exactly." Deborah paused. "Even if these *are* just pranks . . . I feel like I can't jeopardize my campers' safety by putting them in a situation where someone might try something stupid."

I raised my eyebrows. "But the campout is such a big deal to the campers. I know *my* bunk has been talk-ing about it nonstop since they got here."

Deborah sighed. "That's the problem." She looked me in the eye. "You know everything that's happened so far, Nancy, and the whole history. Do *you* think I should cancel it?"

Before I could respond, the mess hall door opened

and Bella stepped out. She glanced at us. "Oh, hi. I just realized I forgot my bug repellent this morning, and I've already got, like, a million mosquito bites. I was just running back to the cabin to get it. . . ." She trailed off, her eyes narrowing as she looked from me to Deborah. "What are you guys talking about?"

"Just a minor incident that happened last night," Deborah said stiffly. "It doesn't concern you."

"Oh, you mean the flooding of Nancy's bunk?" said Bella. "I heard all about it from her campers. That's a real shame, Nancy. Gosh, it's like something's cursing this place this summer, huh?" She tossed her head and headed off toward her cabin, leaving her snarky words lingering in the air.

I watched her until she disappeared into the cabin, then turned back to Deborah. "Don't cancel the campout yet," I told her. "I have a lead."

The sun was high in the sky as Maya and I led our campers through the woods on the southwest edge of camp property. "What other leaves can we find?"

I asked. I already held a fistful of different-shaped leaves that we'd matched to a chart Deborah had given us. So far on our nature hike, we'd seen six kinds of bugs and seven different species of birds, and we'd found poop—we called it "scat" at camp—from a raccoon and a rabbit.

"Here's a funny one!" Cece knelt down and picked up a leaf from the ground that had rounded edges. "It looks like it has polka dots."

Maya ran over. "Oh, cool!" she said. "I think that might be from a sassafras tree. Smell it—does it smell like root beer?"

"It does!" Cece said excitedly.

Maya turned to me. "Nancy, can you hand me the chart?"

"Sure." I took out the folded paper and handed it to my CIT with a smile. It was great to see the girls get so excited about finding new things in nature!

But as most of the girls surrounded Maya and Cece with curious expressions, someone tugged on my wrist. "Hey, Nancy?"

I turned around. Winnie and Katie stood before me, both wearing troubled expressions. "What's up, guys?"

Winnie bit her lip as Katie whispered, "Can we talk to you in private?"

"Sure." I turned back and called to Maya, "Comfort stop!" That's what we said when someone had to use the bathroom on a hike. It was the only reason I could think of for the three of us to separate from the others without questions. Maya nodded that she'd heard me, but kept chatting with the group.

"Come on." I led Winnie and Katie up over a little hill and down the other side, where we wouldn't be seen or heard by the others. "What's going on, guys? From your expressions, it looks kind of important."

Winnie and Katie looked at each other, then back at me. "We have something to tell you," Winnie said.

"What is it?" I asked. I assumed it was going to be something about a disagreement between two of the girls, or some other piece of gossip that Winnie and Katie felt I should know. My bunk got along well, but it seemed like there were always little undercurrents of tension in a group this size. And as BFFs, Winnie and Katie seemed to think of themselves as Friendship Experts.

"Last night?" Katie began nervously. "Before the flood?"

Immediately I became more serious. "You have information about the flood?" I asked. "Did you see anyone?"

Katie looked nervously at Winnie.

"Kind of?" Winnie asked, twirling a lock of hair around her finger. "I mean, it may be nothing. But before the flood . . . like, just a few minutes before . . ." She looked at Katie.

"Something woke me up," Katie filled in. "It was like a thud, probably someone's feet hitting the floor. And I looked around and saw Harper getting up and heading for the bathroom."

I felt a sudden rush of adrenaline. *Harper?* "How soon was this before the flood?" I asked.

Katie shrugged. "I'm not sure, but it couldn't have been long, because I rolled over to go back to sleep, and the next thing I knew I heard Kiki yelling."

I took in a breath, trying to calm my fluttering

heart. Could *Harper* be behind the flood? *But maybe she just had to go to the bathroom.* It was possible. We all got up during the night sometimes. But then I thought, *It actually makes sense that someone from our bunk would have turned on the faucets and showers.* It meant that nobody would have had to sneak in, which would have been difficult. The only entrance to the cabin opened right into the main room with the bunk beds, and the culprit would have had to walk by *all* the sleeping campers, plus me and Maya, to get to the bathroom. Then that person would have had to hope no one woke up from the noise, and sneak past all of us *again* to get back out.

I sighed, and suddenly became aware that Katie and Winnie had been staring at me for a few seconds, waiting for a response. "Thank you for telling me," I said finally, looking at them with sincere gratitude. "I'm sure it wasn't easy. And I'm not sure this means Harper had anything to do with the flood, but I'll look into it. Okay?"

"Okay," said Katie, at the same time Winnie said, "We didn't want to get her in trouble!"

"You haven't," I said, putting my hands on each of their shoulders. "You've just given me some questions to ask. Okay?"

"Okay." Winnie nodded, and Katie did too. After a few seconds, we headed back to join the others.

Harper was holding the sassafras leaf now, studying it with the same intensity she used when she read her beloved books. I watched her, thinking about this new information and going back through all the other events in my mind. *Harper wasn't here when Deborah and I were pulled under. But she was there when Cece and Kiki were . . . and she's a good swimmer. She could have snuck away from the campfire when the sleeping bags were stolen, but that would be a lot for her to do, and get to the lake without being detected. . . .*

As I was thinking, Harper looked up at me and smiled. Struggling to control my expression, I smiled back.

I don't want to believe it could be her. But I need to look into this.

CHAPTER ELEVEN

True Confessions

"HEY, HARPER," I SAID GENTLY AFTER THE hike, as we were all heading back to the cabin for a quick rest before a camp-wide sing-along. "Can we talk for a minute?"

A flash of fear crossed over Harper's face, and I felt the heavy weight of disappointment. *Did she really flood the cabin? If so . . . why?*

"Okay," she said hesitantly, looking from me to the cabin just a few yards away. "Um . . . where should we go?"

I nodded at Maya, to whom I'd given a heads-up that I needed a few minutes to talk to Harper. She was taking the other campers into the cabin to use the bathroom and get whatever they needed for the campfire. She gave me a thumbs-up and headed inside.

"Let's go sit over here," I said, leading Harper to a bench at the edge of the woods, a good distance from any of the cabins. I sat down and patted the bench beside me. It was clearing up after a cloudy morning, and I pointed at the puffy white clouds strewn around the sky. "Pretty, isn't it?" I asked, pointing up.

"I guess." Harper looked where I was pointing only for a moment. She sat down next to me, folded her hands in her lap, and stared at them.

"Harper," I said after a few seconds of silence, "is there anything you'd like to tell me?"

She kept staring at her hands. She shook her head awkwardly but didn't say a word. Still, her tense demeanor told me something was definitely up.

I tried to soften my voice. "The thing is, I know you went into the bathroom last night," I said, "which would be totally normal, except this wasn't too long before we discovered the flood."

Harper still wouldn't look at me. She unfolded her hands, though, and began picking at her cuticles. "Maybe I just had to go to the bathroom," she said after a while, her voice breaking at the end.

"Maybe you did," I said gently, "and I want to stress that either way, you're not in trouble. I just want to talk to you about it."

Harper looked up at me briefly. She looked very young all of a sudden, and very small.

Suddenly her face crinkled up and she started to cry. "I did it," she whimpered, then broke into a sob. "I didn't want to hurt anybody or damage anything. I just thought, if the cabin were flooded, maybe we'd all have to move out and I could go home."

I reached over, gently pulling her closer and putting a comforting hand on her back. "Why do you want to go home?"

Harper leaned into me, resting her head on my shoulder as she took off her glasses and swiped at her eyes with her fist. "Nobody likes me," she cried, her voice full of pain. "My parents wanted me to come to camp to make new friends, and I haven't made any new friends. The other girls are just kind of *okay* with me. I think they think I'm weird." She paused, sniffling. "I'd rather be home with my books and my parents. At least I know what to do there."

I pulled Harper closer, and she let out a fresh round of sobs. I felt terrible for her. My instinct was to try to defend the other girls, who I felt had tried to connect with Harper, but I didn't want to deny what Harper was feeling. *How can I fix this?*

"Harper," I said nervously, "is there . . . anything else you want to tell me?"

She looked up at me, confused.

"Is flooding the cabin the only thing you've done to try to go home?" I added.

Harper's eyes widened. "Oh, yes!" she said. "I wouldn't . . . I mean . . . you must think I'm a monster!"

I shook my head rapidly. "No, no, no, Harper," I said. "I just wanted to be clear. And I think the other girls do like you. Maybe they just don't know you that well? You spend a lot of free time reading, which I know you love, and that's great. But it doesn't give the other girls a lot of opportunity to get to know you."

Harper sniffled again. "They're always busy giving each other pedicures or playing that stupid MASH game," she muttered. I couldn't help smiling, remembering the "future-telling" game (Mansion, Apartment, Shack, House) that Bess had tortured George and me with when we were younger. *I always kind of thought it was stupid too.*

I patted her back. "Tell you what," I said. "How about we skip the sing-along and have a little get-to-know-you bunk meeting instead?"

Harper drew back immediately, looking at me with concern. "I'm *not* playing Truth or Dare," she insisted.

Oh, Harper. We have more in common than you know. I held up my hand. "No Truth or Dare. Scout's honor."

"We're not scouts," Harper muttered, shooting me a puzzled look.

"Sorry," I said, putting the hand over my heart

instead. "I *promise*. You have my word. Now, will you dry your eyes and come back to the bunk with me?"

Harper looked at me for a moment. She pulled off her glasses again and wiped her eyes, which were still pink and wet. "Okay," she said, putting the glasses back on. "But if I'd still rather be home, can I leave early?"

I tried to stifle my sigh of disappointment. *What to say?* "If you really feel like you can't stay, we'll talk to Deborah and Miles and figure something out," I promised.

Harper nodded and stood up from the bench. "Deal," she said, holding out her hand to shake.

". . . we *all* have something that makes us special," I said to the whole bunk a few minutes later. We were all sitting in a circle on the cabin floor, sweating in the stagnant air. Maya had run to Deborah to explain that our bunk was going to skip the sing-along, and Deborah had said it was okay. "And I think we all have more in common than we might realize at first. For example, Harper and

I realized that we both hate the game Truth or Dare!"

There were squeals of surprise, and a few nods of agreement.

"Oh my gosh, I hate that game too," said Nina in a rush. "It's like, want to do something really embarrassing or tell everyone something you *never* planned on telling *anyone*? It's the worst!"

Kiki pushed her playfully. "Are you kidding? It's *so* much fun!"

Nina shook her head, turning away. "I clearly have nothing in common with you," she sniffed.

Everyone laughed, but Kiki held up her hand. "Not true! We both love to watch *Degrassi* on Netflix."

Nina grinned. "I will grant you that," she said.

"*Anyway*, guys," I said. "My point is that we should all make a real effort to get to know everyone here— even the people you don't *think* you have anything in common with. Because chances are, you have quite a lot in common."

Cece frowned and looked at Harper. "Harper, why do you read all the time?" she asked.

"Yeah," Winnie agreed. "It's *kind* of like you don't want to talk to us."

Harper blushed and looked down at her lap. "It's not that at all," she said. "It's just . . . I don't know. I'm a quiet person. Sometimes when it gets really loud and crazy in here, I just need some time to be in my own head."

Katie raised her chin. "That's called being an *introvert*," she said. "I'm one too! I totally get it, Harper."

Harper looked surprised. "You do?"

Katie nodded. "That's why I like to put on my headphones sometimes," she said, and when Harper looked stunned, she added, "You probably don't notice. But a lot of times when everyone's talking, I'll put on my headphones and just focus on the music and think about whatever. It helps me relax."

I raised a hand. "I feel like that too sometimes," I said. "Like, sometimes? If I'm trying to solve a really complex . . . um, problem . . . I'll try to spend some time alone so I can really *think*. Sometimes I find that hard to do with people around."

Everyone nodded.

"Hey, Harper?" Cece asked after a few seconds. "Would you maybe read us some pages from your books? I've been really interested in learning more since you first told us about them," she said, "but I haven't had a lot of time to read here. Maybe if you read to all of us, we could enjoy them with you?"

Harper looked at me, her cheeks flushed with, I thought, pleasure. "Would that be okay?" she asked.

"Oh gosh, yes!" I said. "In fact, I think that's a great idea. Let's all relax on our bunks and you can read us a story, Harper!"

Everyone jumped up and ran over to their bunks. A couple of girls went to use the bathroom, and Harper ran to grab the first book in the series and open it up to the first page.

As we waited for everyone to come back, Maya sidled up to me. "That was awesome," she whispered. "It went just like we hoped it would!"

After I'd had my private talk with Harper, I'd pulled Maya aside to ask how she thought we should handle talking to the whole bunk. It was she who suggested bringing up the things we have in common that we don't even realize. "Look at you and me!" she'd said excitedly. "We're totally different people, but we both care about these girls like crazy, and we make this amazing team."

Now, slapping Maya five, I couldn't agree more. But as I settled onto my bunk, though I tried every position to get comfortable, I couldn't quite relax.

One mystery solved, a little voice in the back of my head said. *But the bigger culprit is still out there. . . .*

After our meeting, I reported the incident with Harper to Deborah. Deborah gave Harper a stern lecture before dinner, but she was going to let her stay.

"So I guess . . . that mystery is solved?" I told Deborah at dinner. "We know she was behind the flooding."

Deborah nodded slowly, looking around the mess hall. I'd cornered her by the doorway while the runners from each table went to get trays of food for their bunkmates. "And she does seem sorry," she said.

"Yes," I said. She seemed a lot happier after she read to the bunk. And I noticed she was chatting a lot with Cece and Katie on the way over here. Maybe she's finally made the friends her parents wanted her to make."

Deborah glanced over at my table. "Okay. I would like to meet with her privately tomorrow as well to just make sure this doesn't happen again. But it sounds like you're right, Nancy. . . . Small mystery solved, larger mystery still . . . lingering." She frowned.

"At least you don't have to call off the campout," I said.

Deborah nodded again. "That's good," she said, but she sounded a little uncertain.

I felt a little uneasy too, as I settled down to eat dinner. But over pizza and lively conversation with my campers, my worries dissipated. Everyone was in such a good mood! And talk soon turned to the campout itself, which everyone was super excited about.

"Will we all be in a tent together?" Nina asked, looking

around the table. "It won't be as much fun if we have to split up!"

"I think everyone's together," Maya said.

"Yup," I confirmed. "Each tent sleeps eight—so it'll be just like our cabin, but smaller and outside."

The girls chuckled.

"Can we go swimming after everyone goes to sleep?" Kiki asked eagerly. "One of my friends said she swam at night at *her* camp. It sounds so fun!"

As several girls chimed in with enthusiasm, I shook my head. "It's *really* dangerous and against the rules to go swimming without a lifeguard present," I said seriously. "So unless you guys can work on Sandy . . ." I glanced across the mess hall to where Sandy was eating with Sam and Taylor. She sensed us staring at her, and when she shot me a questioning look, I just smiled and waved. All my campers started cracking up.

"We'll start working on her tonight," Winnie announced. "During Night Frisbee."

Night Frisbee was one of the more popular nighttime

sports at Camp Cedarbark, and the camp-wide play-offs were tonight. It was basically just Frisbee golf with glow-in-the-dark Frisbees, but somehow the darkness made it a million times more fun.

We finished up our pizza and topped it off with lime Jell-O for dessert. As Cece went up to get our desserts, I noticed Bella slipping out the front door of the mess hall. *Where's she going?* I wondered. I figured she must have left something in her bunk. Harper, Kiki, and Nina got into a debate about which was the best Jell-O flavor, and while it got a little heated, I was just thrilled to see Harper getting so engaged in a conversation with her bunkmates. I found myself wondering whether she would come back to camp next year. *And will I be here?* Well. That was something I hadn't considered up until that point . . . but I *was* really enjoying my week as counselor.

When dinner wrapped up and the campers began slowly making their way out the front door, my campers were laying out a plan for convincing Sandy to take them night swimming during the campout. Part of me was wondering whether I'd created monsters by giving them the idea . . . but the other part was *really* enjoying their ridiculous plans and hoping that Sandy would say yes! Swimming under a starry sky sounded like the ultimate camp experience. And didn't I deserve to get to try it too—especially if this would be my *only* camp experience?

Well. It will be fun . . . if no one gets pulled under.

The thought sent a shiver down my spine. With the cheerful conversation, it was easy to pretend like all the scary things that had happened this week were over. But *were* they over?

Just then a scream came from just outside the mess hall. "Oh my gosh! FIRE!"

My bunk and I were waiting for the crowd to make its way outside, so we couldn't see what was going on. But looking toward the front door, I could see the campers reacting with horror to something they were seeing on the lawn, and I could see the reflection of something bright and orange in the mess hall windows.

I ran to the doors, pushing my way through campers

and counselors to make my way outside. "Excuse me. I'm sorry. Excuse me!"

Outside the mess hall, I found Deborah, standing and staring at whatever was on the lawn with her hand pressed to her mouth. "Oh no," she murmured. The campers around her were standing back, pressing against the exterior walls of the mess hall, as though they wanted to be absorbed back in.

I looked where Deborah was looking, and my heart squeezed in my chest.

Flames erupted from the ground. It took me a minute to realize that the flames were coming up in the shape of words. Yes, someone had spelled out something in some kind of accelerant—gasoline?—on the grass, and then lit the letters on fire.

GO HOME!

And the flames were licking toward the wooden mess hall. . . .

~✦~

CHAPTER TWELVE

Up in Flames

"MILES, GET THE FIRE EXTINGUISHER!"
Deborah shouted. I turned and saw the camp co-owner
stumbling out of the mess hall. He scrambled back
inside, and I felt a little rush of relief.

So Miles was inside the mess hall. Good. Good. If
he was at dinner with the rest of us, that meant he
couldn't have lit the fire. Or at least . . . it made it
less likely.

A hand suddenly shot out and shook my shoulder.
"Nancy!" Deborah cried. "Get the campers back inside
the mess hall. We can't have them running around an

open flame. And with them inside, it will be easier to put this out."

Right. "GUYS!" I screamed, wrapping my hands around my mouth and turning toward the campers. "Everyone back in the mess hall! Come on! Let's stay safe while the fire is put out!"

The campers began slowly making their way back inside—no one seemed eager to give up their prime viewing spot—as Miles came running out, a huge fire extinguisher in his arms. He pulled the key out and aimed the nozzle at the fire as I waved the campers back into the mess hall. "Come on, guys. Come on. Let's let the grown-ups handle this."

Once everyone was back inside the mess hall, the volume soared as everyone began discussing the action outside.

"Who would *set* that?"

"What did it say?"

"It said 'Go home!'"

"OMG, why?"

A small part of me felt like I should be discouraging

this kind of conversation, but I didn't know how. I mean, there were huge flames licking across the camp clearing. Everyone had seen them. There was no denying that something big was going on.

The feeling I'd had at dinner—that *maybe* all the weird happenings were over, for now—completely disappeared. I felt like I'd been plunged into freezing-cold water after a soothing massage.

Bess began leading her campers over to where Maya and I stood with our bunk. "You saw it?" she whisper-hissed to me. Across the hall, I could see that George and Janie were struggling to comfort several of the younger campers, who'd started crying.

I turned back to Bess and nodded. "Go home," I whispered back. "*That* isn't good."

I'd filled Bess and George in on my discovery about Harper that morning. "So someone more dangerous than Harper is definitely at work here," she whispered, too low for any of the campers to make out.

"Yes," I agreed. "And whoever it is just changed elements—from water to fire."

Deborah or Miles must have called the fire department, because within a few minutes of all the campers being sent back inside, we heard sirens, and a huge red fire truck could be seen parking in the camp driveway. Most of the fire was out at that point, but firefighters still poured out and began dousing the remaining flickers. Desperate to keep the campers from panicking, the other counselors and I organized a mammoth game of one of the campers' favorites, Fruit Basket Upset.

It felt like hours before Deborah came back in and announced the fire was out, but it was probably only thirty minutes or so. Her face looked drawn, and she didn't make eye contact with anyone as she stared straight ahead and announced, "I'm sorry, but we're going to have to call off the Night Frisbee play-offs tonight. All campers will go back to their bunks and have ninety minutes of free time before lights-out."

The mess hall erupted in whines and complaints. George's seven-year-olds all began crying louder—even the ones who'd pulled themselves together in the thirty minutes or so we'd been back inside.

"I can't *believe* this!" Kiki said. "We spent all week killing it in Night Frisbee! Now we don't even get our chance at the championship?"

I patted her shoulder. "Sorry, kiddo," I said. "Though you *could* look at it as, now everyone who would have played in the play-offs is a champion."

Kiki sighed deeply. "No. I wanted to destroy the eleven-year-olds!"

"Maybe Harper can read us some more from her book during free time," Maya suggested diplomatically. "Kind of like a bedtime story?"

Most of the girls seemed pleased with that idea. By the time we all filed out of the mess hall and headed toward our cabins, most of the grumbling had stopped—in my bunk, at least. But a haze of disappointment lingered over the whole group.

George brushed up against me as we crossed paths walking to our respective cabins. "Do you think the campout will happen tomorrow night?" she whispered.

I realized I hadn't thought about it—but it was hard to imagine. "I doubt it," I whispered back. "This seems like a pretty clear threat. But I didn't hear that from Deborah, so I don't know for sure."

George nodded solemnly.

"Some of my little kids might be relieved," she said, "but I imagine the rest of the camp will freak out."

"I know," I said, "but better a camp-wide freak-out than some other scary thing happening."

George shrugged. "True. Anyway, have a good night, Nance."

I squeezed her arm before she walked away, then was startled by a cool voice behind me.

"Too bad about Night Frisbee, isn't it?"

I turned and looked into the darkly made-up eyes of Bella. In the dim light of dusk, her face was half-covered by shadow.

"It's a shame," I replied neutrally.

Bella moved closer. "What's a shame is that you

and your goody-two-shoes friends wouldn't let me hold my séance before camp even started," she hissed, too quietly for the campers around to hear. "If I'd been able to communicate with this angry spirit, maybe we could have avoided all this."

As Bella tossed her hair and stalked off toward her cabin, I stood frozen and watched her, stunned. But not by the snotty comment. I was stunned by Bella's smell.

When she'd moved in close to me, it was unmistakable: Bella *reeked* of smoke.

The next morning, about fifteen minutes after breakfast, I stood at the edge of the woods outside Walnut Cabin. Full of nervous energy, I peeked inside the window, but the lack of lights inside made it hard to see anything. Besides, I knew that no one should be in there. I'd seen Bella, Susie, and all six eleven-year-old campers on the soccer field just moments before. Deborah was letting the Night Frisbee play-offs happen this morning, and while the girls were disappointed that it was during daylight, they were all excited to play for the championship.

I'd asked Maya to keep an eye on the girls while I sneaked away "to the nurse for some aspirin" . . . but really, to get inside Walnut Cabin while Bella and her campers were gone.

I hadn't run my suspicions by Deborah. She hadn't canceled the campout yet, but she'd told me this morning that she planned to announce after lunch that it was canceled. It was just too risky, she said. There was no doubt now that someone was sabotaging the camp. And it scared her to bring campers to an unprotected location while that was going on.

I was hoping that I'd find something in Walnut Cabin to prove that my hunch about Bella was more than just a hunch. She'd been strangely obsessed with the "ghost" story since we showed up, and she was capable of pulling off all the attacks. If I could find something inside Walnut Cabin that connected her to the crime . . . then maybe the campout could go on as planned, and without the threat of more strange happenings.

I took a deep breath and darted around to the entrance, pushing open the heavy wooden door and slipping inside. The cabin was dim, and it took my eyes a few seconds to adjust after being in the bright sunlight. When I could see again, I saw a cabin that looked a lot like ours, in terms of the general chaos and the items scattered around. Sleeping bags were spread out on each of the bunks, with pillows and sometimes extra blankets or stuffed animals. There were postcards and stationery stacked on one dresser, and a few dog-eared copies of the Hunger Games trilogy on another.

I stepped over to the bunk beds near the door, in the same location as the ones in our cabin where Maya and I slept. Traditionally, the counselors seemed to take the bunks closest to the door. I walked to the dresser at the foot of the bed and idly shuffled through some items on the top: a necklace with a pendant shaped like a key, a tube of cherry-red lip gloss. *This looks like Bella's stuff.* Then I noticed a postcard peeking out from underneath a pair of sunglasses. I pulled it out and looked down. *Hey, goofball* . . . I skipped the message and looked down at the signature. *Bingo.*

It read *Truly, Bella.*

So I'd accomplished goal number one: locate Bella's belongings. Now I just had to search them.

Casting a quick look out the cabin window—the clearing still looked deserted—I threw open the top drawer and started rifling through it. It was full of underwear and socks, and based on the size, they looked like Bella's and not Susie's. I was about to close the drawer and move on when my fingers brushed something small and hard in the rear corner of the drawer. Taking it in my hand—it was small enough to fit in my palm—I drew it out of the drawer and looked down.

What I saw made my stomach drop. *Matches.* As in, something that might have been used to light the message on the grass last night—*GO HOME*—aflame.

I took in a breath, trying not to get ahead of myself. We weren't supposed to keep matches in the bunks, but realistically, there were lots of reasons a person might have them. Then I remembered Bella's séance attempt. She had had matches then, and she'd put them back in her bag after I'd taken her Ouija board and candle. I picked up the matchbook, examining its surface. The striking strip seemed scratched, like it had been used.

I threw the matches on top of the dresser and pulled open the next drawer. *Maybe I'll find something in this drawer that will make everything clearer.*

But that drawer just seemed to be filled with tank tops and T-shirts. The next drawer held shorts and jeans. And the next one . . . two bathing suits, a sparkly minidress, and a beach towel. But again, just as I was about to close the drawer, I saw something else.

And gasped.

There was something crammed way in back—something hidden from plain view when you opened the drawer.

Is Bella trying to hide something?

I reached in and nearly recoiled. *Hair!* The silky strands tangled between my fingers as I grasped the thing and pulled it out. . . .

Only to find myself holding a long silver wig.

I was so surprised, I dropped it.

I remembered what Kiki had said when she got pulled under. She claimed the person doing the pulling had *long, silvery-blond hair.* Just like Lila had . . . and Bella certainly seemed interested in the incident with Lila.

I picked up the wig with shaking hands. *Why would Bella do this?* Trying to scare campers and counselors in the water, stealing sleeping bags, setting the clearing on fire? What did Bella have to gain if Camp Cedarbark failed? She was a counselor here, after all. She was a Camp Larksong alum, who claimed to love the camp.

I didn't have any answers. But gathering the matches and the wig, I moved toward the door.

And tripped over a pair of black Chuck Taylors. I picked one up—the tracks matched the ones I'd seen the night the sleeping bags were stolen. And they were too big to belong to the campers.

I headed out of the cabin.

I *definitely* had enough to share my suspicions with Deborah.

"I think I may have our culprit."

Deborah looked up in surprise as I made my announcement while opening the door to her office.

"Just like that?" she asked.

"Just like that," I replied. "Well, I haven't figured out her motive yet. But I'm pretty sure the person trying to sabotage Camp Cedarbark is"—I paused, and Deborah's eyes lit with excitement—"Bella."

I went over everything I knew: Bella's strange behavior when we'd arrived at camp, her concern with the "ghost" story and wanting to hold the séance. I explained how Bella didn't have an alibi for any of the strange happenings—she'd excused herself before the swim tests, could have easily snuck away from the campfire when the sleeping bags were stolen, could have snuck away from whatever she was doing when two of my campers were pulled under during their swim time, and I saw her sneak out of the mess hall when the fire was lit in the clearing. Plus, I added, she reeked of smoke later that evening, and I'd found the matches and wig in her bunk. It felt pretty clear that she was the Camp Cedarbark saboteur.

I was expecting the camp owner to look surprised. But instead she looked away, thoughtful, and then gave a rueful little laugh. "Bella. Oh, of course."

"Of course what?" I asked. *What does Deborah know that I don't?*

Deborah shook her head and sighed. "I should have *known* not to hire someone who had ties to this camp! It was silly of me."

I was getting frustrated now. I could feel my eyes bugging out. "Ties to this camp? *What* ties to this camp?"

Deborah looked at me, her eyes apologetic. "Nancy, I should have told you. I'm sorry. It just never occurred to me that there could be a connection." She paused, leaning her elbows on her desk. "Bella's family tried to buy Camp Larksong a couple of years before we did. Her family wanted to renovate it and reopen it too. But their financing fell through."

I stared at Deborah, putting all that together in my head. *Bella's family wanted to buy Camp Larksong?* That could explain why she seemed to know so much about the Lila incident. And if she succeeded in scaring everyone away . . . ruining Camp Cedarbark's first year . . . maybe she thought the camp would go back on the market for a cheaper price? Or maybe her goal didn't even go that far. Maybe she just wanted to get revenge on the people who'd succeeded where her family had failed.

"Bella was a Camp Larksong alum too," Deborah said. "Maybe she decided that if her family couldn't have the camp, no one could."

I let out a sigh. Even though it all lined up, there was something unsatisfying about this conclusion. *It was all about money? Or revenge?*

"Why do you think she focused so much on the Lila incident?" I asked. "Was she involved somehow? Did she have an ax to grind?"

Deborah looked at me blankly. "Well, you're the amateur detective, Nancy," she said. "But from my perspective? She just wanted to convince people the camp is haunted. Because then people would get scared, and eventually, the camp would fail."

I frowned, thinking that over. It made sense, of course. And that explained why Bella told us the story right away and wanted to hold a séance the night the CITs arrived. She was setting up the story that an angry ghost lived at the camp.

Deborah suddenly stood. "Let me get Miles. The eleven-year-olds are at the lake now. Sandy and Susie can keep an eye on them while Miles brings Bella back here. We're going to have to work something out for tonight. Maybe Sam can take over as lead counselor."

I raised my eyebrows. "Wait—you're bringing Bella here? Now?"

"Of course." Deborah looked at me like she couldn't believe I wasn't following this. "She can't *stay* here, Nancy. Not when she might be putting campers in danger." She paused. "The only good news is . . . I guess the campout tonight can go on."

• • •

"Ex*cuse* me?" Bella sputtered about half an hour later.

We stood in Deborah's office. Miles said that Bella had not been pleased to be escorted back to camp in front of all her campers. She'd seemed even less pleased to find me waiting for her in Deborah's office. And when Deborah began explaining why she'd been brought there, I thought her eyes might roll right out of her head.

"Where's your proof?" she asked now, crossing her arms over her chest in a defensive posture. "Why on earth would I try to sabotage this camp? I came here when I was a kid! I love it here!"

I briefly explained what I'd already told Deborah. With every word that came out of my mouth, her eyes looked harder and angrier.

"And I found these in your bunk," I said finally, gesturing to the book of matches and the wig that now sat on Deborah's desk.

Bella let out a rueful laugh. She looked so angry and tense, I was ready for her to explode.

"Do you know why I have matches?" she asked.

"And why I smelled like smoke last night? God, Nancy Drew, what kind of detective are you?'

I stared at her. "Because you . . . started the fire?" I asked, thinking it was pretty obvious.

"*Nooooo!*" Bella lifted her finger into the air and waved it in my face. "I've been burning sage to purify our cabin and keep the angry spirits out." She turned to Deborah, her expression changing from furious to hopeful. "That's what I was doing last night, when the fire must have been lit! I know it's not really allowed, so I try to do it when no one else is there. I went back to the cabin as soon as I finished dinner and burned some sage. That's why my clothes smelled like smoke later. But I didn't see anything, I swear."

Deborah looked unconvinced. "That doesn't explain the wig, Bella. Or the sneakers."

Bella sighed. "The *wig*. I brought the wig for the same reason I brought the sparkly dress. I was going to get all dressed up for the end-of-camp party," she said.

Deborah raised her eyebrows. "End-of-camp party?"

"Don't you remember?" Bella asked. "The kids at

Camp Larksong always talked about this big costume party the counselors had after the kids left at the end of the week. I figured, since it was a Camp Larksong tradition, we'd be doing the same at Camp Cedarbark."

Deborah closed her eyes. "I remember," she said. "But the end-of-camp dance was called off the last year of Camp Larksong because . . . well, because. I didn't plan to keep the tradition going here. I'm not sure why you would just assume we'd be having the dance."

"I *told* you," Bella said. "Because I thought Camp Cedarbark would be the same as Camp Larksong. And I wanted to be prepared."

"Why *silver*?" I asked, not bothering to try to hide my skepticism. "You just happened to bring a silver wig and not, say, pink or blue or any color *not* worn by a fake ghost in the lake?"

Bella looked at me like she was almost afraid. "I have no idea what you're talking about," she said. "I wore that wig for my Halloween costume two years ago. I thought it looked really cute on me. That's all."

"What about the sneakers?" I pressed.

Bella looked at me with disdain. "You mean the same Converse sneakers every other teenager in America wears? Yeah, that's some real incriminating evidence there."

I glanced at Deborah, wondering whether she was buying this. Her expression told me she wasn't. "I'm sorry, Bella," she said after a few seconds. "But I just don't believe you. I'm not going to press charges, but I want you to leave this camp immediately. Call your parents from this phone to pick you up, and I'll escort you over to pack your things. I can't put my campers at further risk. I *can't*. And if you try anything to further sabotage this camp, I will call the police."

Bella shook her head like she couldn't believe this. "You have no proof!" she cried. "I'll sue you! We'll sue!"

Deborah looked tired. "If you want to sue me over losing one day of your summer job, Bella, have at it. But I'm afraid you still have to leave." She began walking toward the door, and I stepped aside to let her pass. She took Bella's arm as she passed her and said, "Come on."

Bella glared at her, then turned her ferocious stare on me. "I won't forget this, Nancy," she said in a low voice. "If our paths ever cross again . . . Mark my words, you've made a lifelong enemy!"

With that, she whirled around and followed Deborah out of the cabin. I watched them walk across the clearing, past the burnt *GO HOME* message in the grass, and toward Bella's cabin.

Well, I thought, straightening up as the words *lifelong enemy* replayed in my mind, *you certainly won't be the first.*

CHAPTER THIRTEEN

Stormy Night

"ARE WE ALMOST THERE YET?" KIKI ASKED, grabbing my arm and walking up beside me. "Just kidding! Ha-ha! Remember the first day when we hiked to the creek, what wusses we were? *This* feels like nothing now."

I smiled, but I couldn't quite agree with her. We were making the long hike up Hemlock Hill to the site of the camp-wide campout, and my legs were burning. Of course, some of my tiredness might just have been from the fact that it had been a long day for me. After Bella's parents came to pick her up—*they* hadn't seemed terribly thrilled by Deborah's decision either—I'd had lunch with my bunk and a session of serious friendship bracelet-making. It was only about five o'clock, but I felt ready to climb into my sleeping bag and say good night to this day.

"I think we *are* almost there now," I said, "but yeah, point taken, Kiki."

"You guys are *so much stronger* than you were!" cried Maya excitedly. "You've grown so much this week! I can't believe you're all going home tomorrow. We have to keep in touch."

Harper rolled her eyes. "Don't get all sappy, Maya," she said. "We still have tonight."

At that moment, I caught a snippet of conversation from the eleven-year-old group in front of me. Sam, who'd taken over Bella's position as of lunchtime, was patiently repeating the story she'd told about fifty times since Bella's departure. "She just urgently had to go home," Sam said. "I told you guys, everything's fine, but it was unavoidable. She wanted to say good-bye, but she couldn't. Don't worry, though—we'll still have fun."

"Why do you always wear that baseball cap?" one of Bella's campers, a redhead named Haley, asked.

Sam grinned, touching her fingers to the brim. "Because it keeps the sun out of my eyes," she replied. "Plus, it looks so darn good on me. Yankee blue is my color, don't you think?"

About ten minutes later we finally came upon the clearing on a rocky ledge above the lake where we'd be camping that night. Each bunk was given thirty minutes to set up their tent and lay out their sleeping bags inside. I'd been worried that it would take longer than that to set up, but actually, with all eight of us working together, setting up the tent was a breeze. It made me realize what a great team the eight of us had become, and that made me smile.

Once our bags and sleeping bags were laid out inside, we headed over to where Deborah and Miles were setting up a campfire. While Miles used a flint to get the campfire started—a cool trick he'd tried to teach the campers—Deborah asked the counselors to line up the insulated bags of food we'd brought. I plunked down the bag I'd gotten from the mess hall, which included hot dogs, buns, potatoes for roasting, and apples. Soon each of the kids was holding a hot dog on a pointy stick over the roaring campfire, and we'd all wrapped potatoes in aluminum foil to roast in the fire.

I hadn't realized how hungry I was until I began to smell the hot dogs cooking, and then my stomach rumbled angrily.

"Hungry much?" George asked, sidling up beside me.

I smiled. "I guess so," I admitted. "Things were still so crazy at lunch, I don't think I ate a lot."

I'd filled George and Bess in on the Bella incident during free period.

George patted my back. "Don't feel bad about it, Nance. You got a crazy person out of here! You saved the campout! Look at all these happy faces that would have been sad, watching another DVD in the mess hall or something."

I looked around at the happy campers, trying to feel the truth in George's words. But something just wasn't sitting right.

"What if she *didn't* do it?" I asked.

George turned to me, her eyes flashing. "Nancy, come on. You can't be serious. Bella was acting weird since the moment we all got to camp."

I sighed. "On the hike up here, I was noticing how many people wear Chuck Taylors," I said. "Sam has them. Maddie too. *Deborah* even has a pair. What if I—"

"Don't doubt yourself," George insisted. "Except about your hot dog, because that thing is about to burn to a crisp. Come on, put her there."

George picked up a paper plate with a bun on it and held it out to me. I pulled my hot dog in from the fire—it *did* look a bit well-done, now that I inspected it—and dropped it on the bun. George handed me the plate, then gestured to a row of condiments that had been set up by a tree.

"You had plenty of reasons to blame Bella. Maybe one or two of them could be explained in other ways—but all of them? No. So eat something," she encouraged me. "Enjoy yourself! You solved the case!

Now you can relax and enjoy a freshly roasted hot dog with a stellar view."

I nodded, slathering my hot dog with mustard and ketchup and moving over to where my bunk had gathered on an overturned log. Soon the happy chatter and jokes of my campers took my mind off Bella, and any of the other crazy events of the week. *George is right,* I thought as I enjoyed my dinner. *The hard part is over—now I can enjoy the little time I have left!* The sun setting over the lake *was* beautiful. And it was hard to ignore what a good time all the campers seemed to be having. *They really would have been disappointed if this had been called off,* I realized.

But the night wasn't going to be *totally* perfect. We'd just finished up our dinner and started roasting marshmallows for s'mores when the sky suddenly darkened, and a huge crash of thunder sounded.

I looked to Deborah, who turned to the sky just as the heavens seemed to open up and rain came pouring down in a gush.

"*Auuuuughhh!*" half the campers screamed.

"Everyone run to your tents!" Deborah shouted. "Take cover! I'll put out the fire!"

"You heard her, guys! Come on!" I corralled my campers into a clump and navigated them back toward our tent. Once we got the zippered flap open, we all tumbled in with a groan and scooted over to our respective sleeping bags.

"I can't believe it," Maya said, shaking her head. "Was it even supposed to rain tonight?"

"Who knows?" I asked with a shrug. "I haven't seen a weather report in a week."

For a few minutes, we just sat in the darkness listening to the rain pounding the roof. The tent seemed to be waterproof, thank goodness, so except for a few small puddles where there were leaks, we stayed dry.

After a few minutes we brought out our flashlights and made a circle in the middle of the tent. Thunder was still crashing every few minutes outside, and lightning would light up the sky.

"It's so cool," Cece whispered. "Like nature is having a big argument."

Harper bit her lips. "I think it's a little scary," she whispered.

Maya scooched over and put her arm around Harper. "Don't be scared," she said. "We're all here together, and nothing's going to hurt us. We should enjoy the show!"

"We should tell *ghost stories!*" Kiki said suddenly, and several of the girls spoke up to agree.

I glanced at Harper. "Maybe we're not all in the mood for ghost stories," I suggested. "Actually, I brought a deck of cards. We could play—"

Harper shook her head and sat up straight. "No, Kiki's right," she said. "The atmosphere is *perfect* for ghost stories."

Kiki beamed. I glanced at Maya, who shrugged.

"Okay?" I said. "Are we all sure, though?"

All the girls grunted their assent. When I looked Harper right in the eye, she nodded.

"Okay," I said finally. "Who wants to start?"

"I do!" Nina raised her hand. "This is a ghost story I heard here, actually. It's perfect because it's about *this camp*."

I sat stock-still as Nina began telling the others about the last year Camp Larksong was in business. How everyone went on the end-of-year campout, right here, at Hemlock Hill. But one of the counselors was acting a little weird. . . .

"Guys!" I said, holding up my hand. "Hold it right there, Nina. I just want you all to know . . . this story *isn't true*. Okay?"

Nina looked at me, slightly annoyed. "How do you know that?" she asked.

"Because I know," I said, hearing that I sounded like a frustrated parent, but not sure how to avoid it. "I . . . looked into it. None of this is true, guys."

I'd expected that to dampen the campers' enthusiasm for the tale, but it seemed to have the opposite effect. Fourteen eyes widened as seven faces turned curiously in my direction.

"You *looked into it*?" Katie echoed. "That sounds kind of serious."

I shook my head, but Cece was already chiming in, "Yeah, I thought this was just a made-up story! But if

Nancy heard it and did some research, there must be *some* truth to it, right?"

The girls' voices all began to drown one another out, and I looked desperately at Maya. But even as I did, I realized that *she* didn't know the whole story either. I'd given her a brief synopsis of Bella's tale the night she arrived at camp, and told her it wasn't true. But she didn't know that I'd found out what really happened to Lila. She didn't know that someone actually *had* nearly drowned on this night five years before—but it was an accident.

"So what happened?" Winnie asked eagerly, clutching the stuffed wiener dog she slept with each night to her chest. Her face was bright with anticipation and a little bit of fear. "Did someone die?"

Nina turned to Winnie, her eyes sparkling. "In the middle of the night, when everyone was sleeping, the counselor took one of the campers outside," she said, "led her down to the lake, and . . . *drowned her*!"

Winnie was the first to scream, and then suddenly the whole tent was enveloped with shrieks.

"Guys!" Maya cried, pushing her hands down through the air in a *calm down* gesture. "Come on, guys. It's just a story. Right, Nancy?"

"It . . ." I was about to confirm this when I suddenly caught sight of Harper. She'd been sitting behind Kiki, who was waving around dramatically, so I didn't see until then how utterly *terrified* she looked. Her skin was as pale as marble, and her eyes appeared glassy. She was trembling hard enough that I could see it from several yards away.

Suddenly we heard footsteps outside the tent and the hatch was unzipped. This sent the girls into another round of screaming, all except Harper, who sat utterly still. A flashlight beam shone in, at first obscuring the person behind it, but then Sam came into focus.

"Everything all right in here?" she asked. The rain was still lashing down outside, and Sam was getting soaked. I felt terrible for letting my bunk get so excited and disturbing her. "We heard you guys way on the other side of the clearing. George says you're freaking out the little ones."

"I'm sorry, I'm sorry," I said, trying to stand in the cramped tent. "The girls were telling ghost stories, and it got a little out of hand."

Sam raised her eyebrows. "Ghost stories are fun, but maybe you girls should move on to bedtime-y stories," she suggested. "It's getting pretty late. The little ones were already trying to sleep, and we're bedding down soon."

"Good idea," I agreed.

Sam nodded, smiled, and backed out of the tent. She zipped up the flap behind her.

Suddenly Maya spoke. "Hey, Harper," she said, reaching over to place a gentle hand on Harper's arm, "did you bring your book? Maybe you could read us another chapter."

"Yeah!" cried Cece, bouncing up and down.

"Another chapter, another chapter!" the other girls began to chant.

Harper still looked a bit dazed, but she shook her head, as if to snap herself out of it. "Sure," she said quietly after a few seconds. "Let me just get it from my backpack."

She did, and Maya handed her the powerful flashlight she'd brought to use as a reading light.

Soon Harper took us all to a fantasyland where unicorns kept the peace, dreams were used as currency, and a friendly dragon gave advice to humans. Harper's soft voice against the pelting rain made for a super-soothing story. We all climbed into our sleeping bags, and even I felt my eyes drooping.

When Harper reached the end, she said, "That's the end of that chapter," closed the book, and put it by her pillow. Then she settled into her own sleeping bag. She looked much calmer than she had during Nina's story.

"Good night, everyone," I called, snuggling down. About half of the girls were asleep already, but the rest called, "Good night," and in what couldn't have been more than thirty seconds, I was fast asleep.

A silver-haired girl moved soundlessly through the forest, slipping through the trees like a breeze. She looked behind her nervously, like she feared she was being followed. Then she moved into the clearing, which opened out onto a black, mirror-smooth lake.

An owl hooted as she ran to the beach and silently slipped into the water. The cool water enveloped her quickly, but she had no problem staying afloat, or seeing in the bright moonlight. A single silver beam cut through the water, illuminating something on the black lake bottom. A shining pearl ring.

The girl's eyes widened and she dived down to retrieve it. It slid easily into her hand, and for a moment she just stared at it, the pearl reflecting in her velvety black eyes. She smiled, relieved. Then, just as she cupped the ring in her hand and lifted herself in the water to swim back to the surface . . .

Something grabbed her around the neck. *It was dark, a creature made of shadow and fangs, and it pulled her toward it, screaming. Alarm flashed in her eyes; she knew she was going to die. The ring fell from her hand. . . .*

And I woke, my heart pounding a mile a minute.

"Nancy! Help!"

I gasped, terrified, trying to make sense of the darkness around me. *Oh, right.* I was in a tent with my bunk. It was the end-of-year campout. I must have just been having another nightmare. I tried to breathe in, to calm the hammering in my chest. *I guess that ghost story affected me more than I thought. . . .*

Then I remembered: Someone was calling for my help! Or were they? I listened hard but heard only silence. Even the rain had stopped.

Was I just hearing things?

I reached for the small flashlight by my bed and turned it on. I flashed the weak beam around the tent, counting each sleeping head: *Maya, Kiki, Cece, Winnie, Katie, Nina . . .*

And one empty sleeping bag.

I leaped up, angling to get a better look. Harper's book still lay by her pillow, but the sleeping bag was rumpled and unzipped, as though she had recently left. I sat up, trying to quiet the clenching feeling in my stomach. *She probably just got up to use the bathroom. It was raining and we didn't go before bed.*

Now the woods were silent. The rain seemed to have stopped.

As quietly as I could, I slid out of my sleeping bag and crept out of the tent. I briefly considered grabbing Maya's higher-powered flashlight, but then decided against it. *I'm only going to be a minute. She's probably right on the edge of the woods, using the latrine we dug.*

Outside the tent, the clouds had parted to reveal the moon, which was only a razor-sharp-looking crescent. I breathed in the cool night air and felt a bit better. *Nothing to worry about.*

I shone my flashlight on the narrow path that led away from the tents and into the woods. The latrine was just a few yards beyond the first trees. As I got closer, I heard human-sounding noises and felt a rush of relief wash over me. *She's just using the bathroom. No big deal.*

I moved closer. "Harper?" I called, shining the flashlight toward the tree we'd dug the latrine behind. "Are you okay?"

"Hey!"

A voice that was decidedly *not* Harper's cried out

in alarm. "A little privacy, maybe? I'm not Harper! Sheesh!"

In my surprise, I couldn't place the voice at first. But then it came to me. It was Janie, Bess's CIT—aka Mini-George.

I backed away, feeling my cheeks burn. "Sorry about that! Sorry!" I stumbled back along the path to the cluster of tents in the clearing.

But if that isn't Harper . . . where is she?

I was trying to quiet the fear that seemed to fill my veins with ice when I heard the voice again.

"Help me, Nancy! Please!"

It was undoubtedly Harper. And it was coming from a narrow path that led up the hill, farther into the woods.

I felt my heart speed up as I moved toward the path. I shone my weak flashlight beam ahead, but it barely penetrated the inky-black darkness. *Just like in my dream,* I thought.

And just when I thought I couldn't be any more afraid, a hand reached out and grabbed me from behind.

CHAPTER FOURTEEN

~∞~

A Deadly Plan

BEFORE I COULD SCREAM, THE FIGURE that had grabbed me spoke. "Nancy, what are you doing?"

I shone my flashlight beam at it and nearly collapsed with relief. "Bess!"

She pushed a thick lock of blond hair behind her ear, still frowning. "What's going on?" she asked. "Why are *you* out here?"

"Because I'm missing a camper," I replied. "And—"

"You too?" Bess's eyes widened. "I'm missing Janie, and—"

"I found Janie," I replied. "She's using the latrine and doesn't want to be bothered. But Harper—"

"It's not just Janie," Bess said quickly. "Though that's a relief, that she's okay. I'm missing Olivia, too."

Olivia. I pictured the tiny girl with dark braids who liked to follow Bess around like a starstruck duckling.

"She'd never wander out on her own," Bess went on in a rush. "She's not the type. So I'm worried—"

"Help me please! Pl—mmmmph!"

My head swung around in the direction of the path. This time it sounded like Harper's voice had been muffled, like someone had pressed a hand over her mouth.

"I was about to tell you," I said quickly to Bess. "It's coming from this path . . ." I shone the light up the path, just barely illuminating any of the darkness.

"Great," Bess said, shining the flashlight from her smartphone in the same direction. "Let's go."

But as much as I wanted Bess's company, I knew she could be more help here. "No, you stay here and wake Deborah and Miles," I hissed. "Then the three of you follow up this path as soon as you can. Okay? I don't have a good feeling about this." I swallowed hard. "I'm afraid I was wrong about Bella," I added, and then, when Bess nodded, started up the path.

My flashlight barely illuminated more than two feet in front of me, and the tiny sliver of moon wasn't much help. The path was steep and rocky, and I mentally scolded myself for stupidly passing on Maya's brighter flashlight. But it was too late now.

I followed the path up and around a steep bend, from which I could look down at the clearing filled with tents below. I could see light coming from Deborah and Miles's tent. *Bess must be telling them.*

I shone the flashlight ahead and kept going.

Now I was almost hoping to hear another cry for help. It would tell me that Harper was still okay and clue me in to her location. But only the soft chorus of bugs and frogs greeted me as I wound along the path, and the occasional deep hoot of an owl.

Are they okay? Does that mean they're not *okay?*

I wasn't sure how long I'd been walking. Ten minutes? Fifteen? I'd rounded the hill, and the path was now taking a slow descent back toward the lake. My chest tightened as I looked at the black, glossy surface of the water, remembering my dream.

If whoever's behind this is the same person who's been sabotaging the camp . . . and they're obsessed with what happened to Lila . . .

I had to stop myself from finishing the thought.

Harper is a good swimmer, I reminded myself instead.

I just hoped the same could be said for poor little Olivia.

There was only silence on the path behind me, and I wondered what had happened to Bess, Miles, and Deborah. Weren't they coming? Surely they would come help, right?

Suddenly I reached a tiny clearing in the path, a small rocky outcrop that stood high over the lake. A small beach was below and to the left. I shone my flashlight all around, but couldn't see where the path led from here. Down to the beach? Back into the woods? I'd gotten completely turned around and wasn't sure where the tents were from here. Worse, I hadn't heard anything from Harper or anyone else in at least ten minutes. My heart pounded. I hadn't seen any branches leading off this path, but it was certainly possible I'd missed one or two in the dim light.

"Harper?" I called into the silence.

Then my flashlight died.

"SUCCOTASH!" I screamed.

Stupid, stupid batteries. My spares were in my dresser back at Juniper Cabin.

With my tiny beam of light gone, the darkness seemed to close in on me. Could I even find my way back to camp? The path was winding and rocky. It had been hard to follow even *with* the light.

I took in a shaky breath. *And Harper—where is Harper?*

That was when I heard a muffled cry.

It was coming from my left.

"Hello?" I called. Squinting, I could make out a tiny clearing in the woods to the left, with a bench in the middle. As my eyes adjusted to the darkness, I started searching the dark woods all around.

And nearly felt my heart stop when I made out four pairs of eyes reflecting the weak moonlight.

I heard a *crunch* and then a shriek of pain. Then Harper's voice: "Nancy! I knew you would come!"

"Who's there?" I called, stepping closer. Two other pairs of eyes were at Harper's height or lower, but the third figure was big, as big as me. And it was standing in an odd position, with the kids clutched to its sides. Its hands seemed to be covering their mouths. . . .

"So you found us," the larger figure finally spoke, and the sound startled me enough that I couldn't place it at first. But then, suddenly, it clicked. I moved close enough to make out more detail, and sure enough—

A Yankees cap.

"Sam!" I cried. "What on earth are you doing!"

"She took us!" Sam must have been startled enough by my appearance that she let go of Olivia's mouth, and the girl's squeaky voice suddenly sounded from Sam's side. "I got up to go to the bathroom and she grabbed me! And then we waited a few minutes, and she grabbed Queenie and Harper too, the same way!"

I moved forward hesitantly. "Why did you do that, Sam?" But the truth is, I was afraid of what she'd say. There was no *good* reason to steal three campers and force them into the woods above the lake, on the anniversary of Lila's near-drowning. . . .

Sam moved forward, out of the cover of the trees, and suddenly reached up and pulled off her Yankees cap. In the thin moonlight, out spilled a pile of silky, silver-blond hair.

I gasped.

"Lila is my sister," Sam said simply, her eyes shining with a feral glow. "And this is our revenge—on Camp Cedarbark and on Deborah!"

I sputtered, caught off guard. "But—but—Lila survived!" I managed finally. "I looked into it! She had some neurological damage, but she recovered, and she's alive and well!"

Sam narrowed her eyes. "Sure, *she's* alive and well," she said. "But what about me?"

What? I glanced at Harper and the other girls, and they looked just as confused as I felt. "What about . . . *you?*"

"Lila's my older sister," Sam went on. "Have you ever thought about what your life would be like if such a huge accident happened to your sister? The effect it would have on your parents?"

I didn't have siblings, but I tried to imagine. "Er, not . . . good?"

"Not good at all!" Sam advanced on me, making me shrink back, but then she stopped and seemed to catch herself. "I grew up in a prison, Nancy. I wasn't allowed to have playdates, or go swimming at the beach, or climb on the high bars, or pretty much any-thing." She snorted.

"But . . . what does that have to do with Camp Larksong?" I asked. "Or Camp Cedarbark? Or Deborah?"

Sam sneered at me. "Are you seriously asking me that question?" she asked. "Deborah was *responsible* for Lila's accident. She was her counselor. She failed to convince Lila that they'd find the ring later. She didn't notice when Lila snuck out of the tent, and then she failed to save her."

I stared at Sam. "It was an accident," I said. "Even counselors can't prevent everything, Sam. She didn't realize how upset Lila was and didn't hear her get up. Is that really an offense worth all this?" I remembered Harper's flooding of the bunk. I'd failed to notice how upset she was *before* it happened. It seemed like Deborah hadn't done anything worse the night of Lila's accident.

Sam glared. "*Someone is responsible, Nancy,*" she said in a low, creepy voice. "And someone is going to pay." She turned from me to the girls, who were huddled together, shivering. Her eyes took on a wolfish glow.

I suddenly became very aware that Bess, Deborah, and Miles were nowhere to be seen. "Pay . . . how?" I asked. *Maybe I can keep her talking. Just keep her talking and give them a chance to find us so we can overpower her.*

Sam tossed her head. "By ruining any chance of Camp Cedarbark being successful," she replied. "That's why I applied to be a counselor here—under a different last name. Deborah never suspected a thing. And so I've been sneaking into the lake and pulling people under," she went on. "I've spent the last six months training myself to hold my breath for five minutes! Plenty long enough to get out of sight and take a breath. That also allowed the campers—and *you*—to experience what it must have felt like to be Lila."

I shook my head. "Lila went under *herself*," I pointed out. "No one pulled—"

"*Shut up!*" Sam moved closer, a vicious expression on her face, and I fell silent. "That's why I stole the sleeping bags and dumped them in the lake. And, when no one seemed to be listening, that's why I set my message aflame in the main clearing. GO HOME—and forget this camp. Never come back! Horrible things happened here!"

I was shivering now, just like the girls. *Sam is crazy*, I realized. Whatever real problems she had, it was clear she wasn't capable of thinking rationally about this. Which made her capable of a lot of very scary things. I listened hard but couldn't hear anyone approaching. "What . . . are you going to do now?" I asked, struggling to hide the fear I was feeling.

Sam smiled. "A few missing campers should dampen the enthusiasm for Camp Cedarbark," she replied. "And if I dump them in the lake? All the better. People will remember Lila and know that something is evil here."

Something sure is. A chill ran up my spine. "You can't hurt these girls," I said. "They've done nothing to you!"

Sam laughed—a hollow, insane laugh. "I've done nothing to anybody either!" she cried. "But my parents treat me like an invalid. Listen. I *can* do whatever I need to, to get my message across. But you know what?" Her eyes took on a satisfied gleam. "A *counselor* missing— that would really be the icing on the cake."

She stepped forward. Trembling, I stepped back.

And back.

And back.

"What are you doing?" I asked, trying to sound tougher than I felt. "Are you going to attack me?

Because I may look small, but I'm scrappy! I could take you!"

Sam snorted. "Could you?" she asked.

I looked her in the eye. "I've taken on worse than you," I said. And that was true.

Sam laughed that same hollow laugh again. "The thing is, I won't even have to do the work," she said, nudging her chin toward something behind me. "The fall would kill you. You'll probably hit your head on one of those big rocks, and then . . . *splash*."

My blood chilled. I looked behind me and inhaled a silent scream: Sam had backed me up just inches away from the rocky drop that led down to the lake. She was right: the fall was steep enough, and rocky enough, that I probably wouldn't survive it.

Even in the dim moonlight, I could see that.

I closed my eyes. *Please, Bess,* I prayed silently. *Please, anyone . . .*

CHAPTER FIFTEEN

~❦~

A Sad End

"NO!" I CRIED, AND MY VOICE SHOOK A little. "How does killing one random counselor punish Deborah? It punishes my family! My dad—" My voice broke at the thought of Dad. Or Hannah. Or Ned. *Might I really never see them again?* I forced their images out of my mind and thought, *Keep her talking.*

"I don't care about your family," Sam said simply, moving closer, "just like Deborah didn't care about mine."

The girls were advancing behind Sam, watching the action with wide, terrified eyes. I realized this was their chance to escape. "Girls! Get help!" I cried. "Run back to camp. Tell someone—anyone!"

The girls moved forward, and Harper looked at me regretfully, the moonlight shining off her glasses, like she couldn't decide whether to leave.

"I mean it," I whispered fiercely. *"Go."*

With one final look in my direction, the three girls scampered down the path.

Sam moved even closer as the girls disappeared. "I hope you really enjoyed your time as a counselor, Nancy," she said, her lips parting in a terrifying smile. "I hope it was a great final act."

I listened as hard as I could, hoping against hope to hear Bess, Deborah, and Miles. But all I heard was a dull *clink*—probably one of the girls kicking a rock on their way back to camp.

I took one more step back and felt my heel hit a rock. I was at the end. I closed my eyes, trying to squelch my fear. *Stay alert. Stay in the game.* I knew it was my only chance of surviving.

I felt rather than heard Sam advance one more time.

And then, suddenly, the night air was cut by her scream. "AAAAAAUUUUGH!"

I opened my eyes to see a shadowy shape grab Sam's legs and plunge something sharp into her calf. Dark blood oozed up from the wound, and Sam fell backward.

"AAUUUGH! What are you doing?" she shouted.

I felt frozen but forced my legs into motion and scampered around Sam and my savior so I was no longer backed against the edge of the drop. As I stared at the tangle around Sam's legs, I recognized Harper—minus her signature glasses!

The sharp thing she'd stuck into Sam's leg was still in her hand, covered with blood. It was a broken lens from her glasses.

"Harper, thank you!" I cried.

Then, before I could say more, I heard voices coming up the path.

". . . think I heard them up here," Bess's voice came from the trees, and then she, Deborah, and Miles burst into the clearing.

I stared at them, overwhelmed with relief.

"I'm so sorry," Bess blurted as soon as she spotted

me. "We took a wrong turn right out of the clearing and got totally turned around . . ."

"What happened here?" Deborah asked, taking in the scene with a stunned expression.

I leaned down and pulled Harper toward me, away from Sam, who was crumpled on the ground hugging her leg. "Ouuuuuch!"

"I'm not sure you'd believe me if I told you," I said, "but I think we've found Camp Cedarbark's ghost."

"*What* a story," George breathed the next morning, as we lounged on benches in the clearing that separated our cabins. "I have to admit, I figured something shady was going on at the camp . . . but I never could have put that together."

"I'm just relieved it's not a real ghost," Bess murmured, scratching a bug bite on her arm. When George and I both turned to her with surprised looks, she shrugged. "What!" she cried. "I'm not saying I always believe . . . but that thing in the water was pretty creepy."

"It sounds like Sam has real problems," George said, looking thoughtful.

I nodded. "Yeah," I said. "I heard Deborah and Miles turned her over to the police, but they recommended counseling. She was nearly catatonic when they brought her back to camp."

"Maybe medication would help," Bess said.

"I hope so," I admitted. I wasn't about to forgive Sam for trying to kill me any time soon . . . but I wanted her to get better. I realized she wasn't in her right mind.

It seemed like Bella had been telling the truth, after all. . . . She really hadn't done anything wrong, except burn some sage. I still wasn't sure why she was so interested in the "haunting," but then I didn't understand why Bess watched that Kardashian show either. And I was sure Bess didn't understand why I loved solving mysteries. I guessed we all had weird interests, when it came down to it.

I knew I owed Bella a huge apology. I was still trying to figure out the best way to do it.

The door to Juniper Cabin opened and out spilled my campers, all carrying their sleeping bags and luggage. They threw everything into a pile beside the cabin and I glanced at the camp driveway, where buses were already waiting. A few cars full of parents were lined up too. I couldn't quite believe it, but my campers were headed home.

The girls came running up to me in a stream, with Maya, who'd been supervising the packing, following behind them.

"Nancy, I need a hug good-bye!" Kiki cried, wrapping her arms around me.

"Me too!" Cece added, running up behind her.

"Thank you for taking care of us!" Winnie said with a grin.

I wasn't sure the campers understood the full scope of what had happened the night before—and that wasn't a bad thing, in my mind. They knew that Harper had left camp and I'd gone after her. Deborah had brought Harper, Olivia, and Queenie back to the main camp, where they'd spent the night with Deborah in her safe, locked house. They were all shaken up, but otherwise unhurt. Sam had been brought to the camp nurse, then taken off in an ambulance. She was in a nearby hospital while her parents and the police discussed next steps. Everyone else, including me, Bess, and the rest of the campers, had stayed at the campout site until morning. With the threat removed, Miles saw no reason to move the entire camp back to the cabins in the middle of the night.

The campers had been told that Sam had a breakdown and had to go home. They hadn't been told about her plot to hurt the girls, or me. I had no problem with that. Knowing wouldn't make them any safer, and would probably scare them.

I hugged each of the girls in turn. The last was Harper, who stood squinting without her glasses. I gave her the hardest hug of all, not sure what to say to her that could possibly express my gratitude.

"I made you a gift in arts and crafts," Harper said into my shoulder as I squeezed her.

"*You* made *me* a gift?" I asked, amazed. "It's me who owes you."

Harper shook her head. "I could have had a terrible time here," she said, "but you looked out for me. You helped me get to know the other girls. That's why I did what I did, Nancy. Not everyone cares as much as you do."

I felt my eyes tearing up and pulled Harper closer in a hug.

"Here," she said when I let her go. She pushed a sheaf of papers at me.

It was a small homemade book, with a cardboard cover decorated with ornate illustrations. CAMP CEDARBARK was the title. I flipped it open and gasped. The handwritten narrative told the tale of all our adventures at camp—minus the craziest one last night.

Harper looked sheepish. "I finished it yesterday," she said, "so it leaves some things out."

"That's probably fine," I said with a smile. "Thank you so much, Harper."

I gave her another huge hug.

"We have to get on the bus," Harper said, "but can we get your address, Nancy? I'd like to write you letters."

"Letters?" Cece chuckled. "What is this, 1985? How about *e-mail*?"

"You can't draw on e-mail," Harper said with a shrug.

I handed out little sheets I'd printed up for the campers with my snail mail and e-mail addresses. "Here you go," I said. "I hope I hear from all of you! I'll really miss you guys."

"Me too," said Maya, handing out her own little slips. The girls took them eagerly and exchanged hugs with her, too.

"Thank you for being such a great counselor and CIT," Winnie said. "We'll really miss you both!"

After a bunch more hugs and promises to keep in touch, the girls hefted their bags and took off running for the buses. There, Miles helped them load their luggage in the back and climb on. I waved furiously as they all boarded the steps, then disappeared from view.

I felt a tear trickle down my cheek.

"It's crazy, isn't it?" Maya asked, moving over to

stand beside me. "We only knew them for a week. A *week*," she said.

"It feels like forever," I replied. "And I hope they will keep in touch."

Maya smiled. "You'll keep in touch with me, too, right?" she asked.

"Of course," I said sincerely, smiling.

As we spoke, Janie and Marcie were running over from where they'd been saying good-bye to Bess and George. They both carried their luggage and sleeping bags. Maya turned back toward the cabin and picked up hers, too.

"Are you leaving already?" George asked, stepping up behind me. "You guys aren't taking the bus, are you? I thought those were just for campers."

"They are," Marcie replied. "But Maya's dad is giving us all a ride."

"Yeah!" said Maya excitedly. "It turns out we all live within fifteen minutes of each other."

Janie nodded. "We've already made plans to meet up for a slumber party in a couple of weeks," she said.

"We really want to stay in touch after school starts."

We all hugged our good-byes, and I whispered to Maya that she really had to write me e-mails, or I would cyberstalk her. Maya just smiled and told me I had nothing to worry about—I would get *sick* of her e-mails. I told her that was very unlikely.

Once we had all said our farewells, the three CITs grabbed their bags and ran over to the same cool convertible Maya had arrived in. A man I assumed was her dad was at the wheel, I saw, and he tooted his horn in greeting. All three girls piled in and waved to us as the car drove away.

"Amazing," said George as we watched them go.

"Truly," said Bess.

I smiled. "Well, I hope Mini-Nancy, Mini-George, and Mini-Bess become as good friends as we are," I said. "And I hope their friendship lasts just as long."

Bess and George looked over at me warmly.

"Hear, hear," said Bess, raising an imaginary glass.

"However," George piped up, raising a finger, "I hope that if Mini-Bess comes to Mini-Nancy and

Mini-George with the really *awesome* idea that they should all be counselors at a semi-haunted camp in the wilderness, Mini-George and Mini-Nancy will have the good sense to say no."

Bess feigned an outraged look and swatted George. "Come on! We had fun!"

We all broke up laughing.

"We did," I agreed, looking over the now-quiet cabins with a sigh, "but it will sure be good to get home!"

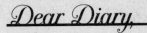
Dear Diary,

OKAY, SO TROUBLE *DID* FIND ME, BUT it was worth it to get to know my fantastic campers, especially Harper. I'm so happy that she was finally able to settle in and make a few new friends.

I do feel bad for Sam. If only she had realized earlier that hurting other people never makes right an old wrong. Scaring the Camp Cedarbark campers didn't solve any of her problems! I hope she changes her ways—and that her family and friends will be able to get her the help she needs.

READ WHAT HAPPENS IN THE NEXT MYSTERY

IN THE NANCY DREW DIARIES,

The Ghost of Grey Fox Inn

"WHAT DO YOU THINK, GIRLS?" I CALLED to my best friends, Bess Marvin and George Fayne. "Should we drive with the top up, or down?"

Bess twisted to look back at George, who was sitting in the backseat of the white convertible we'd just rented from Charleston International Airport. "That's a silly question, Nancy," George said. "It's eighty degrees, the sun is shining, and we're on vacation—put the top down!"

I grinned and pushed a button on the dashboard to lower the car's roof. The South Carolina sun was a welcome change from the stormy late-summer weather back home in River Heights. "It's perfect weather for a wedding!" Bess exclaimed, taking a pair of tortoise-shell sunglasses out of her purse.

"It certainly was nice of Charlotte to give you 'plus two' for the wedding, Bess," I said, pulling onto the main road toward town and enjoying the wind blowing through my hair. "Otherwise, we wouldn't have been able to have this little getaway together." Bess's cousin Charlotte was getting married in two days, and she had invited Bess to be one of her bridesmaids. Because Charlotte was marrying a handsome news anchor, the wedding was all over the news and the Internet—everyone was calling it the wedding of the year. George and I were delighted to come along—maybe we'd even be able to squeeze in a little time on the beach!

"I can't wait for you guys to meet Charlotte," Bess said. "The girl is so organized, I bet she's got the entire wedding planned down to the millisecond. I wonder what color she's picked for the bridesmaids' dresses? I never got a chance to ask. A warm peach would be perfect for this time of year—or maybe cranberry!"

I could almost hear George rolling her eyes from the backseat. "What does it matter? It could be lime green or neon orange—boys would still be falling over themselves to talk to you."

"Lime green?!" Bess exclaimed in horror. "Ugh. Well, Charlotte isn't exactly a fashion bug, but I think she'll have picked something more suitable than that."

I shook my head and smiled. Bess and George may be cousins, but they couldn't be more different. I glanced over at Bess, who looked like an old-fashioned movie star, with her dark sunglasses on and her blond hair tucked neatly back into a silk scarf. Bess had been gushing with excitement about this wedding ever since she got the invitation a couple of months ago. Besides all the hype, both families were fairly wealthy, so it was bound to be quite the elegant affair. And more than that, Bess simply loved the romance of it—the flowers, the dresses, the music . . . everything.

George, on the other hand, couldn't have been less interested in the idea of attending a wedding. Charlotte was from the other side of Bess's family, so George wouldn't know anyone there. Even so, she was all too happy to travel to a new city and check out the sights. Wedding or no wedding—it was an excuse for an adventure. Peeking in the rearview mirror, I spied George taking pictures of the passing landmarks with her smartphone, her short black hair flying in the breeze. She was dressed in jeans and a thrift-store T-shirt—the official George Fayne uniform for every-day comfort.

"Check it out!" George called suddenly. "It's Rainbow Row!" I slowed the car as we drove up to a line of beautiful row houses painted in pastel colors.

"Ooh, look at that powder-blue one," Bess cooed. "And there's a pink one too!"

George madly snapped photos until we'd passed the last house, when I stepped back on the gas. "I was hoping we'd get to see that!" she said excitedly. "Did you guys know that Charleston is the oldest city in South Carolina? People often call it the Holy City because of how many churches there are here."

"I guess that makes it a really good place for a wedding," I said, stopping at a red light.

"And because it has such a long history," George added, "it's famous for having a lot of ghosts! Even the place where we're staying is supposedly haunted."

I raised my eyebrow at this and craned my head to look at George. "Did a lot of web surfing on the plane, did you?"

George smirked and held up her hands in surrender. "Guilty as charged, Sherlock," she said. "Another baffling mystery: solved!"

I chuckled as we continued driving through the picturesque streets of historic Charleston. George loves to tease, but the truth is, to me, mystery solving is anything but a joke. Back home in River Heights, I've gotten somewhat of a reputation as an amateur detective—and over the years I've learned that trouble has a way of finding me, no matter where I go.

"There it is!" Bess said, and pointed toward a stately white building up ahead. "The Grey Fox Inn!"

I pulled the convertible into the curving driveway

that led to the inn's entrance, and stopped the car to take in our surroundings. The building had two stories, with wide, columned patios wrapping around the entire first floor. The grounds were taken up with lush, sculptured gardens, dotted with stone bird fountains and overlooked by huge, moss-covered trees.

"It's absolutely stunning," I breathed.

"I just hope they have Wi-Fi," George said, jumping out of the car.

As we were pulling our bags from the trunk, a blue sedan came up the driveway and stopped behind us. A petite brunette popped out of the backseat and squinted at us through black-framed glasses. "Bess!" the young woman said. "Oh, I'm so glad you're here!"

Bess smiled widely and ran over to embrace her. "I wouldn't miss it for the world!" Bess took the girl by the hand and pulled her toward us. "I want you to meet my very best friends, Nancy Drew and George Fayne—George is my cousin from the other side of the family back in River Heights. Girls, this is my cousin Charlotte Goodwin—the bride-to-be!"

I reached out my hand to Charlotte, who grasped it firmly, looking me straight in the eye. It was strange—given my two friends, I would have thought Charlotte to be one of George's relations rather than Bess's. Her dark brown hair was cut in a no-nonsense, chin-length bob, and she wore no jewelry aside from the sparkling diamond on her ring finger. Her somber maroon turtleneck and black pants seemed completely at odds with the light and summery city all around us. "Thank you for coming all this way," Charlotte said seriously. "I know it's a long trip from River Heights."

"The pleasure is ours," I replied. "Thank you for inviting us to your big day." I cocked my head as a sweet scent reached my nostrils. "Huh," I said. "What is that smell?"

"Oh," Charlotte's cheeks reddened. "It must be this perfume I'm wearing. It's too strong, isn't it? I hardly ever wear the stuff. I can wash it off if you—"

"No, not at all!" I interrupted. "I was just going to say how nice it was." After her initial delight at seeing

Bess faded, I noticed that Charlotte seemed anxious and pale. Was something wrong?

Bess must have noticed too. "You doing okay, Charlotte?" she asked, stepping closer to her cousin.

Charlotte looked startled by the question. "Me? Oh—of course. Why wouldn't I be?" She paused and wrapped her arms around herself, as if she were chilled even as the blazing sun beat down on our heads. "I just . . . I guess you can never really be prepared for something like a wedding," she continued in a low voice. "It's so stressful! Getting all these different people together, hoping they'll get along. And there'll always be something that you didn't plan for—"

"Charlotte!" a voice called from the blue sedan. "Where do you want all these gift bags?"

"I'll be right there!" Charlotte replied. She turned back to us, all business once again. "Some of the other bridesmaids are helping me get everything out of the car," she said. "But you guys go ahead and check in with the front desk; I'll see you inside. Your rooms should all be ready." She started to step away, but then stopped and turned back to us. "Oh! I almost forgot." She reached into the tote she was carrying and pulled out three gift bags. "These contain maps of the area, with restaurants and other attractions clearly marked, as well as some miscellaneous toiletries, in case you forgot anything at home. I included a few historical pamphlets for light reading as well." She handed a bag to each of us, gave a sharp nod, and turned to help her friends unload the car.

"Wow," I said, peeking into the meticulously packed bag as she left. "You were right, Bess. She is organized."

"This is classic Charlotte," Bess replied with a wave of her hand. "She's always been a very serious person, even when she was a little girl. She's pursuing a PhD in history, you know. That's what brought her to Charleston in the first place—and how she ended up meeting her fiancé, Parker. To be honest, I was surprised to hear that she was getting married. She never seemed like the kind of girl who was interested in romance!"

"The right person can turn anyone into a romantic," I said, thinking of Ned, my own boyfriend back home.

We hauled our suitcases up to the front patio of the inn, where several guests reclined in wicker rocking chairs, sipping tall glasses of iced tea. We crossed the threshold into the main foyer, and all stopped to gape. A grand, curving mahogany staircase dominated the room, the steps carpeted in scarlet. The walls were papered in a faded floral print, and the wooden floors shone in the sunlight that poured through the large windows at the rear of the building.

"Not too shabby," George said appreciatively.

"Oh . . . there are Charlotte's parents—Aunt Sharon and Uncle Russell!" Bess said.

A group of people were clustered around a small central table, which had been laid out with glass pitchers of iced tea and tiny sandwiches. The couple I guessed were Mr. and Mrs. Goodwin were both lean and well dressed, and Mrs. Goodwin sniffed at the sandwiches as if she wasn't sure whether to trust them. Bess had told us that Charlotte's family lived in

Connecticut—her mother was a real estate agent, and her father worked on Wall Street.

Also standing at the table was a handsome young man with ash-blond hair, dressed in a cream-colored linen shirt and oxford shorts. An older couple stood on either side of him like bookends, a stark contrast to the Goodwins. Unlike Charlotte's parents, these two were short and stocky people; the man had an ostentatious mustache, and the woman wore her bleached-blond hair in a bouffant that looked as if it were hair-sprayed within an inch of its life.

"Well, Parker," the older man was saying, "aren't you going to introduce us to your new in-laws?"

"Sure, Dad," Parker replied, a little awkwardly. He gestured to Mr. and Mrs. Goodwin, saying, "These are Charlotte's parents, Russell and Sharon."

Parker's father stepped forward and pumped Mr. Goodwin's hand with fervor. "Welcome to Charleston, y'all. The name's Cassius Hill—but my friends all call me Cash."

"It's a pleasure to meet you, Mr. Hill," Mrs. Goodwin

said, a little stiffly, and extended her hand to him.

But instead of shaking it, Mr. Hill brought her hand up to his lips and kissed it. "The pleasure is all mine, madam," he said playfully.

I watched as Mrs. Goodwin's face paled.

"Allow me to introduce my lovely wife, Bonnie," Mr. Hill said. Mrs. Hill moved to stand next to her husband, her light blue, flouncy dress fluttering around her as she went. "Forget the handshakes," she said in a heavy Southern drawl. "I'm a hugger!" She threw her arms around the startled Goodwins, just as Charlotte came through the door and saw what was happening.

"Oh," she said, clearly dismayed. "I see you all have already met."

"Yes," Mr. Goodwin said, extricating himself from Mrs. Hill's embrace. "We have."

"And they say Yankees and Southerners can't get along!" Mr. Hill chortled, a little too cheerfully. The joke was greeted with a stony silence.

Mrs. Hill cleared her throat and looked around the

room, seemingly searching for something to talk about. Her eyes landed on the girls and me. "Now, Charlotte, who are these lovely young ladies?" she asked, stepping toward us.

Relieved to have the focus off her flustered parents, Charlotte pointed us out in turn. "This is Bess Marvin, my cousin—she's going to be one of my bridesmaids. And these are her friends George Fayne and Nancy Drew."

Mrs. Hill nodded politely at Bess and George, but her eyebrows went up a little when she took a closer look at me. "A redhead!" she said, almost to herself. And then a little louder, "How very nice to meet you all." She moved back to the table with her husband and son. Parker began pouring iced tea for everyone, while Mr. Hill regaled the Goodwins with the history of the inn. As he was talking, Mrs. Hill surreptitiously rapped her knuckles three times on the surface of the table. If I hadn't been watching, I would have missed it completely.

Parker saw it too and came over to me with a drink. "Don't mind her," he murmured with a smile. "My mother is extremely superstitious, and this whole wedding thing has her on high alert for bad luck."

"But what does that have to do with Nancy?" George asked.

Parker looked apologetic. "Well, redheads are sort of like black cats. If one crosses your path . . ."

Bess laughed. "Well, Nancy is known to attract mischief wherever she goes!" She went on to tell Parker a little bit about my exploits as an amateur detective.